DON'T EVEN GO
THERE

DON'T EVEN GO THERE

BRENDA HAMPTON

www.urbanbooks.net

Urban Books, LLC
78 East Industry Court
Deer Park, NY 11729

ISBN 13: 978-1-60162-244-0
ISBN 10: 1-60162-244-9

First Trade Paperback Printing February 2011
Printed in the United States of America

10 9 8 7 6 5 4 3 2 1

Distributed by Kensington Publishing Corp.
Submit Wholesale Orders to:
Kensington Publishing Corp.
C/O Penguin Group (USA) Inc.
Attention: Order Processing
405 Murray Hill Parkway
East Rutherford, NJ 07073-2316
Phone: 1-800-526-0275
Fax: 1-800-227-9604

Chapter 1

As the saying goes, there are always two sides to every story. There was his side: "I'm sorry, she didn't mean anything to me. Please forgive me." My side, however, was the only one that mattered. If Plan A didn't work, I was sure to have a Plan B.

I sat in my cubicle, filing my nails and thinking about what I had done last night. I would have given anything to see Drake's face up close, but his yelling and screaming at me through the phone was enough to put a smile on my face. Why? Because Drake deserved it.

It all started after I had gone to Norfolk, Virginia to see my father. He has prostate cancer, but don't feel sorry for him, because he has done things to me that a father should never do to his daughter. I returned home early from my trip. I decided to surprise Drake, who had been my beau for the past three years, and showed up at his house unexpectedly. I'd shown up unexpectedly plenty of times before, so not calling in advance wasn't an issue. That, of course, changed last night, when I swerved into his driveway and spotted a gray Acura parked next to his car.

I paced to the door, then quietly inserted my key into the lock. The door squeaked just a little, but the soft music playing was sure to drown out any noise I'd make. The dining room was to my left, and I immediately noticed two tall cream candles that had already been burned. Leftover food was on two plates, and a half-empty bottle of wine was chilling in a glass bucket of melting ice. Drake was doing it big, but there was no doubt that I was anxious to see what was transpiring in his bedroom.

My eyes scanned the T-staircase that led to the upper level, and, one by one, I tackled the carpeted stairs. Midway, I took the tip of my burgundy stiletto to kick aside the lace black panties and bra. I guessed the woman could have been at least a size 11/12 like me, and after seeing "Victoria's Secret" scripted on the tags, she obviously had good taste. To see her underwear dropped on the stairs, I knew there obviously had to have been much anticipation to get to the bedroom. I definitely knew how that was, as Drake was always a spontaneous and creative lover.

When I reached the door, I wasn't nervous at all, simply because I'd warned Drake about something like this ever happening. He knew what kind of woman I was, and if he ever doubted what I was capable of, he'd soon find out.

The double white doors to his bedroom were closed. But from the outside, I could hear the loud moans and groans. You'd better believe he was giving it to her good, and to hear my man ask, "Who does this pussy belong to?" and her reply, "You baby. You know it's you," I was stunned. My perfectly arched brows went up, and as I listened to Maxwell set the mood for them with his lyrics, I cracked the door, peeking inside of the room. All I could see was her long chocolate legs poured over his broad shoulders, and his naked ass tightening with each thrust. The headboard was hitting the wall and the squeaky mattress that he and I had worn out was being put to work. I watched his lips give passionate kisses on her legs, and due to the exchange of loving words, this couldn't be classified as a one-night stand.

With that in mind, instead of doing the obvious, I closed the door and backed away from it. I quickly moved down the steps, causing my long trench coat to blow open. I exited Drake's house, and when I got to my car, I took a deep breath to calm my nerves that had started to rattle. I drove to the nearest gas station, and removed two red gasoline containers from my trunk. I never thought the containers would come in handy, but there was a purpose for everything I'd purchased. I filled the containers with gas, then drove back to Drake's house, slamming my car into park. By then, I was pissed. I was upset because I had just spoken to Drake earlier, and he expressed how much he loved me. He said that he was so lonely while I was away, and asked me to hurry home. He seemed so concerned about my ailing father, and when I expressed my emotions to Drake over the phone, he wished like hell that he could be there to comfort me.

To make matters worse, just last week, he made mention of us getting married. He was so ready to settle down, and I was the woman he had waited a lifetime to find. No doubt, Drake was full of it, but he wasn't the only one. Yeah, some people want you to

believe that there are still good men out there, but
that's a bunch of bullshit. "A good woman can find a
good man" is a lie, and if another person feeds me that
crap, I have one suggestion: you'd better have a Plan
B. To me, faithful men didn't exist, but I was so willing
to give Drake one last chance to prove me wrong. We'd
dated for three years and had begun to talk marriage.
Last night, though, he failed to prove to me that he
was different from all the others, and for doing so,
he'd have to pay.

I got out of my car and doused the front and side of
his two-story house with gasoline. My trail led from
the front door, and stopped when I reached the back
door. The smell of petroleum made me feel high, but
not as high as I was going to feel when I saw this baby
go up in flames. I emptied both containers, then stood
by his front door. I reached for my cell phone, and
after redialing his number three times, he finally answered.

"Hello," he said in a groggy tone, as if he were
asleep.

"Are you asleep?" I teased.

"Yeah, baby, I was," he softly replied. "I just got in
not too long ago, and as soon as I hit the bed, I was
out. I'll call you in the morning, okay?"

I placed a cigarette in my mouth and dangled it
around. "By then, it might be too late," I said.

"What you say? Too late? Too late for what?"

I backed up a bit, lit the cigarette and flicked it in
front of me. Within seconds the fire ignited and started
to blaze around his house.

"Too late to apologize."

His voice was now clear. "Apologize for what?"

"For setting your ass on fire. In a few seconds, that

dick of yours that you can't contain will melt, and so will your porcelain doll who's in bed with you. Good luck with that, honey, and I guess I don't have to tell you never to call me again."

I leaned against my car that was now parked on the street. I saw Drake pull his curtain aside, and his hollering rang out through the phone.

"Hell, nah," he yelled, looking out of the window at me and the growing flames around his house. "What in the fuck have you done? Are you crazy?"

I slammed my phone shut, and jumped into my car. I slowly drove away, but from my rearview mirror, I saw Drake and his slut run out of the house with a little of nothing on. He used a fire extinguisher to try putting out some of the flames, but it was to no avail. By the time I was less than a half a mile away, I could hear the fire trucks en route.

That was last night, and as I continued to think about it while sitting in my cubicle, I placed the nail file on my desk, chuckling from my thoughts. I expected the police to arrive soon, and right before lunch, they did. The receptionist called me into the lobby, and when I got there, two officers, one black and one white, stood waiting for me. The black one couldn't help but check me out. I was neatly dressed in a navy blue, fitted suit that hugged every curve of my hourglass figure. A lime green silk blouse was underneath and it matched my hoop earrings. My hair was in a sleek, weaved-in ponytail that could have been classified as my own. My slanted hazel eyes were said to be addictive, and many thought that I resembled a younger Lynn Whitfield. I had watched her in the movie *A Thin Line Between Love and Hate*, and needless to say, I loved it. She damn sure had her Plan B.

"Cha . . . Chase Jenkins?" the black officer asked, standing in a trance.

"Yes. How may I help you?"

I folded my arms, but the officer suggested that we step away from the receptionist's desk. I swished my hips from side to side, asking the officers to follow me to the black leather chairs in the far corner of the lobby. I took a seat, crossing one long, moisturized leg over the other. My skirt hiked up a bit, and I could only imagine the thoughts that swam in both of the officers' heads. They were all smiles, and their eyes scanned me from head to toe.

"Do you know Mr. Drake Wilkerson?" the white officer asked.

"Yes, I do. He's my ex-boyfriend."

The black officer removed his cap and tucked it underneath his arm. He remained standing in front of me. My eyes flirted with the growing hump in his pants, but when he spoke, I turned my attention to him. "His house was set on fire last night and he says that you're the one who did it. Were you at his residence last night?"

I threw my hand back and sighed. "Officer, Mr. Wilkerson is a very bitter and upset man. I ended our relationship a few weeks ago, and he's had a difficult time moving on. I just returned from a trip last night, and I don't know anything about a fire at his house. From what I do know, though, Mr. Wilkerson has several female companions. Anyone could have been responsible, but I assure you that it wasn't me."

"He says that he saw you outside of his house. Said you called him directly and told him his house was on fire. Did you call him?"

"As a matter of fact, I did. Only because he called

me numerous times, cursing at me and making threats because I ended our relationship. I told him to stop calling me, and I warned him that I would get a restraining order if he didn't. I can't believe he's gone this far, and if he burned his own house to put the blame on me . . ." I paused, blinking away the fake tears rushing to my eyes. "That's just crazy."

The black officer felt sorry for me, and when he reached out to give me a Kleenex that was on the table beside us, I took it. "Thank you," I said, dabbing my eyes. I took another glance at his hump, sucking in my glossy bottom lip.

"You're welcome. And if you feel as if this gentleman is a threat to you, then my suggestion would be for you to take immediate action." The white officer's walkie-talkie went off and he excused himself, moving a few feet away. "As I was saying," the black officer continued. "Take action and handle your business. Don't be afraid to report these kinds of jerks. You really need to be careful."

I nodded and felt relieved. "Do you have a card or any information as to where I can get a restraining order against him? I've never had to do anything like this before, and I'm so afraid of what he'll do."

The officer didn't hesitate. He reached out to give me his card, then advised me to go to the courthouse if I needed to obtain the restraining order. I held his card in front of me, thanking him again for the information he'd provided.

He cleared his throat. "That will be all, Ms. Jenkins. But, if you ever want to use my card for your personal use, you can. Have a good day, and I hope to hear from you soon."

I stood and gave no reply to what he'd said. All I did

was nod, and walked away with all the confidence in the world. When I got back to my desk, everyone was being nosy, trying to find out what was going on. Even my boss, Liz, was standing by her office, waiting for me. She couldn't wait to question me.

"Everything is fine," I said, entering my large cubicle. "The police wanted to question me about my exboyfriend. His house was set on fire last night, and the police had to make their rounds to see if I had anything to do with it. I told them that I was out of town, so that cleared my name pretty quickly."

Liz smiled and sipped from her cup of black coffee. "How dare they come up here asking for you? You would never do anything so ridiculous and your ex should feel stupid for even mentioning your name."

"I agree."

Liz rubbed my arm, then told me to get ready to join her in our eleven o'clock department meeting. I was her secretary, which was a downgrade for me. I had a degree in business administration, but with the economy being so bad, I had to find a job that would help pay the bills. Liz wanted me to take the minutes in our meeting, so I gathered my thick note-pad to do so. My other coworker, Claudette, looked over her cubicle and into mine. She was always being so damn nosy, and I despised women like her. Plus, she thought that God had blessed her with the best man ever. She had pictures of the two of them inside of her cubicle and displayed on her computer monitor. They had taken plenty of trips together. She'd always come in bragging about how much fun they had, and where he was taking her to next. The day he proposed to her, we couldn't get a darn thing done at work. She rambled on about how much she loved him, and he loved her. When the red roses showed up, I could have choked. She cried, and couldn't wait to call and thank him. I listened in as she told him how much he meant to her and that she couldn't wait to be his loving wife. Everybody was so happy for her, and the people around here couldn't wait to hear all about her business. I never told anybody anything about my personal relationships. They knew I dated, but my business was my own. There were some things Liz knew about me, only because she was my boss. And those things were limited to my age, which was thirty-one, my address, and my salary. My salary was $41,500 a year, and my other two coworkers, Claudette and Veronica, always wanted to know how much I made. We all were very competitive, and with every little thing, we always tried to outdo each other.

Truthfully, neither of them could touch me with a ten-foot pole. Claudette was too darn skinny; her light skin and long hair barely got her by, but I was sure her big lips came to good use. As for Veronica, she was brown skinned like me. She weighed about two hundred plus pounds, and her self-esteem issues drove me nuts. She always had to get approval about how she looked, and the no-good boyfriend she bragged about wasn't helping her self-esteem issues one bit. I'd listened to her cry plenty of times over the phone, asking him why he did this or that to her. It was so ridiculous for any woman to put up with that much mess, and that's why I didn't. You basically had one time to mess me over, and I wasn't in the business of forgiving. Before my mother passed away, she taught me a lot about men. She and my father argued all the time, but she never tolerated much from him. They'd been separated for years, and he was now with his other woman.

When my mother died of breast cancer, I promised myself that I would always live by what she told me. That was to see about me, myself, and I. "Never let a man control you," she said, and I just couldn't do it.

As for my father, he had prostate cancer, but he was hanging in there. I never really had much of a relationship with him, other than when he would come into my room at night and touch me. I told my mother about it, and we got the hell out of there. That's what a woman with Plan B will do, and I disliked my father ever since. Per the suggestion of my counselor, just in case my father kicked the bucket, I thought I'd go see him so it wouldn't be on my conscience if something happened to him. I had no other siblings, but that was fine by me. I was known for being selfish, but that suited me just well. As I said, I was looking out for me, and I suspected things would remain that way for a long time to come.

"Did you check your messages yet?" Claudette asked, still looking over my cubicle. "Your phone was ringing off the hook while you were away."

"I'll check them when I get out of the meeting. Aren't you going in there too?"

"I may be a little late, but I'm coming. Korey is supposed to drop off some money for lunch, so I'm waiting for him to arrive."

I thought our meetings were mandatory, but Claudette was known for having her way with Liz. Now, Liz and I got along pretty well, but all of us could tell that Claudette was her favorite. She was soft-spoken and came off as being polite as ever. Her image was perfect and her work performance was always commended. Mine was as well, but that's because I knew how to put on a good front. I was a Gemini, so therefore I had two sides to me. In no way was I crazy, or anything like that, but I knew when to turn it off, and how to turn it on. There was a place and time for everything. My professionalism was on display at work, but I could turn into the real me at home. I considered myself to be a very nice person, but just don't rub me the wrong way. Drake got a piece of that action last night, and even though I knew it was him ringing my phone at work, I ignored it.

I headed into our meeting, and when I got to the boardroom, at least ten—people from some of the other departments, too—surrounded the round mahogany table with black leather chairs. Everyone was talking, making the room noisy as ever, but when Liz walked in, the noises calmed down. Liz was a black woman in her late forties, but looked good enough to pass for thirty-something. She was slim, very classy, and wore her hair almost cut bald. It was always trimmed to perfection and everyone knew she was definitely about business. She scooted her chair up to the table, and when she flipped open her notes, we knew it was time to be quiet and tune in. She did a quick head count, noticing that Claudette's seat was empty.

"Claudette will be joining us in a minute," she said. "I'm going to wrap this up as quickly as I can, as I know some of you haven't had your lunch." She turned to me. "Chase, if you wouldn't mind going to get all of us some sodas and cups, I'd appreciate it. Also, I forgot my blue folder on my desk. Stop in my office and get it for me, please."

I left the room to retrieve the folder for Liz and grab some sodas from our break room. It was difficult trying to carry the sodas, so I placed them on a tray, along with some plastic foam cups. As I was on my way back to the boardroom, I was bumped by a man who swiftly turned the corner. The tray dropped to the floor and the sodas rolled in different directions.

"I am so, so sorry," he said, bending down to help me pick up the sodas. "Please forgive me."

I had already forgiven him, and as sexy as he was, why shouldn't I have? I already knew who he was, just from seeing the pictures in Claudette's cubicle. Still, I wanted to be sure. He looked a whole lot better in person, and he kind of reminded me of Pooch Hall from the BET show, *The Game.*

"No problem," I said, batting my eyes with long lashes. "Mistakes happen."

He put the last soda on the tray and displayed his pearly whites. "Wherever you're planning to take those, you can't open them anytime soon. Can I help you get some more?"

"If you don't mind," I said. "I got them from our break room, and if I don't get these back to our board meeting soon, I might be in trouble."

Korey chuckled and followed me to the break room. I put it on in front of him, making sure my sexy swagger was on point. I even unbuttoned the single button to my jacket so he could get a closer look at my perfect perky breasts, which were squeezed by my silk blouse. When we got to the break room, I opened the refrigerator and he helped me put more sodas on the tray.

"There you go," he said, swiping his hands together. "Done deal."

The deal was in no way done yet, and I was hooked on his muscles that were bulging from his royal blue T-shirt. His baggy jeans had a sag in the right place and his coal black waves made me seasick. The most addictive thing about him was his smile, and no wonder Claudette couldn't stop bragging about *her* fiancé. He was gorgeous and she should have known that she'd have to share a man this darn handsome.

I held out my hand. "Thanks, uh . . . What did you say your name was?"

He shook my hand. "I didn't, but my name is Korey."

"Well, thanks, Korey. You really were a big help."

"I was going to help you take those to your destination, if you don't mind."

I blushed and waved him off. "I'll be okay. Go ahead and thanks again."

He shrugged, then put his hands into his pockets. As he walked toward the door, I couldn't help but undress him with my eyes. There was no way in hell that Claudette knew what to do with a brotha that fine, and he had to be annoyed by that squeaky voice of hers. I couldn't let him get away from me, and I was willing to accept the rejection—if it came.

"Say, Korey," I said, halting his steps. He turned around. "My name is Chase Jenkins. May I ask you for a tiny favor?"

"Sure," he replied without hesitation.

I picked up a napkin and laid it on one of the tables. I removed my pen from my suit jacket and held it out to him.

"May I have your phone number? I really like what I *see* and I hope the feeling is mutual."

He blushed, and the dimples went into effect. His shyness was too cute, but his hands hadn't moved from his pockets. "I'm involved with someone who works here. Her name is Claudette. Do you know her?"

I shrugged. "Somewhat, but not as much as I'd love to get to know you."

He hesitated for another second, then removed his

hands from his pockets. *Yes!* I was in business. He was a lefty, and he took the pen and scribbled his phone number on the napkin. I smiled with glee in my eyes. Any man could be persuaded and I was glad to know that Korey was willing to be on my team. He dropped the pen on the table, and winked at me on his way out. *Right back at you, honey,* as I'd definitely be calling him tonight. You see, Drake was already history, and it stunned me how I could get over such a tragic loss so quickly. Knowing that he wasn't worth even one tear made it so, so easy to move on. I already had something in the works to look forward to.

Chapter 2

For two weeks straight, Korey and I stayed on the phone for hours. That was possible for us to do because he and Claudette hadn't moved in with each other. Surprisingly, he was a welcoming person to talk to, and had opened up a lot about his relationship with Claudette. According to him, he loved her, but there was something missing. He couldn't really explain what, other than saying that she was the kind of woman his mother always wanted him to have. He was thirty years old, worked with his father selling cars, and had a college degree from the University of Missouri, St. Louis. He kept inviting me to go on a date with him, but I wanted to take my time with this. I started to feel a bit guilty about talking to Claudette's man, but I hadn't expected to indulge myself with the many conversations that we'd had. My intention was to only have sex with him, but I had never been the kind of person to up the goods so soon. There was only one occasion where I had a one-night stand, and the only reason that had happened was because I got blissfully drunk that night. I hadn't been that way since, and even though I remembered the brotha was packing some thick meat, I couldn't remember his name or number. So much for that, but I at least had myself an okay time.

I sat on the bed with the phone pressed up to my ear, holding it with my shoulder. Soft music was playing in the background, and I kept looking at the TV in front of me that showed women from my favorite reality show clowning. The fragrance from a lit vanilla candle stirred around my room that was neat as a pin. Everything from the silk pillows and cream sheets on my queen bed to the soft lavender color on my walls decked it out as if Martha Stewart had come over and done it herself. While carefully polishing my toenails, I talked to Korey over the phone.

"Why are you playing games with me, Chase? I know you want to see me."

"I do, but give me a little more time. I told you I just got out of a bad relationship, and with you and Claudette being engaged, I don't know if this is the right move for me." I knew, I was just playing around with him. Us getting together would happen, but it would happen on my time.

"See, there you go bringing up Claudette again. It is what it is, but if the ring ain't on my finger yet, I really don't see what's the big deal."

Ring on his finger or not, the result would be the same. I didn't say so, but I sure as hell felt it. Before I could respond, I heard hard banging on my door. I pretty much had an idea who it was, as Drake had been trying to get at me for days. He told me he was coming by, and even though I'd gotten my restraining order, he didn't wish to play by the rules.

"Korey, let me call you back. Someone is at my door."

"Why you got that other brotha coming over there to entertain you? That's why you're playing me shady, ain't it?"

"No. Now, I gotta go. Later, all right?"

Korey hung up, with an attitude, too. *What nerve?* I could tell I would have to be careful how I played my cards with him. The banging continued, and as I got off the bed, the wet polish on my toenails touched my plush tan carpet.

"Darn it," I said, looking at the stain on my carpet.

"Chase!" I heard Drake yell. "I know you're in there. Open the door!"

I tightened my silk flowered robe, and waddled to the door with my toes flipped in the air so they wouldn't touch my carpet. I knew the day would come when I would have to confront Drake, so I guessed that today was my lucky day. I pulled open the door, and stood with no expression on my face. From the look of Drake's cold, red, and glassy eyes, I could tell he'd been drinking. He was a borderline alcoholic, but I dealt with that issue. The fact that he was handsome as ever and put me in the mindset of Idris Elba, that kept me attached too. Sex between us was spectacular, but a cheating man I would not tolerate.

Since I'd opened the door, he tore into me. "I hope you have a good explanation for setting my house on fire. There are thousands of dollars of damage, and I expect you to pay me for the damages."

"I hope your insurance premiums were paid up, because I'm not giving you one single penny. Besides, I don't know what you're talking about, and if you came over here to argue with me, please don't waste my time. I've set you free, so let's be done with it."

Drake bumped my shoulder and swaggered his way inside. He wore a leather coat, blue jeans, and black dress shoes. His low-cut fade was neatly lined, and his goatee suited his chin well. No, his looks couldn't be ignored, but seeing him made me think about the woman's legs thrown over his shoulders.

"You are lucky that my insurance premiums were paid up, but for the next month or so, my house is not livable. I have to stay with my brother. Do you have any idea how much you've inconvenienced me?"

I wasn't sure if Drake had a tape recorder, so I wasn't going to admit to any thing. I closed my door and stood in the living room with him. "I'll say it again, Drake, I have no idea what you're talking about. Don't blame me if you got caught with your pants down, and one of your other women got upset with you. That's what you get for trying to be a player."

Without being offered a seat, he took one on my beige sectional. "I wasn't trying to be no player. I dated that chick a long time ago, and when she stopped by to see me, one thing led to another. She knew about you and that was the first time, during our relationship, that something like that happened."

"Save it for your chickenheads, okay? You got busted, and no matter what you say, I'm never going to take you back. I in no way believe that was the first time something like that happened, and at the end of the day, it doesn't really matter."

Drake sat silent for a moment, then stared at me as I continued to stand close by the door. "Okay, Chase, I fucked up. Sorry. We're not going to let three years go down the drain, just like that, are we?"

Drake couldn't be serious, could he? I tried to burn this fool up in his house, didn't I? Why was he apologizing to me? This had to be a joke. I moved closer to the door and touched the knob. "Maybe when you're sober, you'll realize how serious all of this is. Three years, four, or ten, baby, you got busted. What we had is o-v-e-r, and there is nothing left to be said. I'm deeply sorry about your house, but you should have known that there are consequences for men who backslide on their women. When you find out who the woman was who burned your house, let me know. I'd like to send her a thank-you card because she did me a favor."

Drake stood and walked up to me by the door. "Quit playing," he said. "I'll give you some time to think about all of this, okay? You act like you ain't have no damn love for me, and it's not cool that you don't want to work this shit out. I'll get at you in a couple of weeks. By then, maybe you'll have come to your senses."

I said not one more word, and opened the door. Drake could see in my eyes that I wasn't playing with him, and, eventually, he'd have to accept the fact that there would be no reconciliation. He left and I happily slammed the door after him.

That night, I was asleep in my two-bedroom apartment, dreaming about Drake and another woman. When the telephone rang, I jumped from my sleep and reached over to see who it was. It was Korey calling, and I couldn't believe that it was almost 2:30 A.M. *How dare he call me at this time in the morning?* When I didn't answer, he had the nerve to call right back.

"Hello," I snapped.

"I didn't mean to call you so late, but I couldn't

sleep. Do you still have company, or did he already leave?"

Korey was starting to irritate me. Who I had at my place was none of his business. "I'll call you tomorrow," I whispered. "I haven't gotten much sleep tonight and I have to get up for work in a few hours."

He pushed again. "Are you alone?"

"No," I lied. "As a matter of fact, I'm being rude right now. We'll talk tomorrow."

I hung up, and it was official. Korey was scratched from my to-do list, simply because he was already becoming a pain in the ass. All we were was phone buddies, and he was trying to keep tabs on me when he already had a woman. That in no way made sense to me.

I was running late for work, and now I couldn't find my keys. Why was I running late? Because I couldn't get back to sleep after Korey's phone call. I was up thinking about my past relationship with Drake, too, and had started to feel disappointed about the three years I'd wasted with him. What a setback.

I finally found my keys, and as I left my apartment, I bumped into my neighbor, Lance, who was leaving his apartment too. He seemed to be running late as well, and we met up on the steps.

"Good morning," he said, extending his hand for me to go down the steps in front of him. "Ladies first."

"Thanks, Lance." I hurried down the steps in my high heels and thick winter coat. The light snow had been falling for a few hours, and when Lance and I reached our cars, they were covered with snow.

He looked at his watch. "I guess there's no need to hurry because I'm already late."

"Me too," I laughed.

He brushed the snow off his car with a snow scraper and offered to do mine. I had a towel that I'd gotten from my trunk and it really wasn't doing much. I accepted Lance's offer and stood shivering as I watched him clean both of our cars. Lance was just an okay-looking brotha. He looked to be in his late thirties, had a shiny bald head, and wore a trimmed mustache. I could never tell if his body was hooked up or not, because his clothes were always too big and, quite frankly, too slouchy. I had seen several different women at his apartment; I guess it really didn't matter how a man looked, as his collection was always more than one. Besides that, he drove an older model Ford Expedition that needed some work. He was always outside trying to fix it, and had asked me for a jump at least twice. I wasn't trying to judge; after all, Lance seemed like a really nice person.

"You're good to go, Chase," he said, stepping away from my car. "Be careful on the roads and have a good day."

"You too, Lance. Thanks."

I got into my clean burgundy car, quickly turning it on so it could heat up. Lance waved again before pulling away. I followed him, making my way to work.

I was twenty minutes late, and the only person who had made it there before me was my other coworker, Veronica. Her cubicle was behind mine, and instead of peering over it like she always does, she came around it to talk to me. I hung my coat on the coat rack, and her eyes were checking me out.

"You always look so nice in your suits. How many of them do you have? I swear I've never seen you wear the same thing twice."

I was a clothes and shoe fanatic, but I knew how to coordinate my outfits to make them look different. The gray pantsuit I wore today was accented with a silk pink blouse and silver and pink accessories. My sleek ponytail was flipped on the ends and my makeup was a work of art. I understood why Veronica seemed jealous.

"You know how much I love clothes, but you look cute too," I lied. The flowered skirt was not working for her and she looked like a blooming fat petunia. The hip-length sweater she wore was too tight, and if Veronica would have glanced in the mirror a little longer this morning, she would have seen what I did. Aside from that, she did have a pretty, round face, and her natural hair was full of tight curls.

"Thanks for the compliment, Chase. I guess we'll have to wait for Liz to get here. She already called and said she'd be about thirty minutes to an hour late. I got an early start, so traffic wasn't a problem for me."

"Well, it was for me." I nudged my head toward Claudette's cubicle. "Did she call in yet?"

"No, not yet. I'm sure she'll be showing up soon. She hasn't missed one day of work."

As Veronica spoke, I got a closer look at her. I noticed a small bruise close by her eye, and squinted before questioning her. "What's that underneath your eye?"

Instead of saying anything, she walked over to her cubicle and pulled out a compact mirror from her purse. She touched the bruise with her finger, then pulled out a tube of foundation to dab the spot underneath her eye. "Stupid me," she said. "I bumped into my door yesterday and hit my eye. I didn't know it had gotten that bad and I tried to cover it up."

I knew what Veronica said was a lie, and this wasn't the first time I'd noticed a bruise on her face. I couldn't help but confront her about my suspicions. "Veronica, you don't have to lie to me, all right? I suspect that your boyfriend has something to do with those bruises that I keep seeing on you. You really need to leave him alone, especially if he's putting his hands on you. If there is anything that I can do to help, let me know."

Veronica's eyes had already started to water. I reached out to give her a hug, and gave her a Kleenex that was on her desk. She dabbed her eyes. "We get into it all the time over stupid stuff. I try to keep my mouth shut, but he always calling me names and saying things that hurt my feelings. I do fight his butt back, but there's no doubt that he always gets the best of me."

I shook my head with disgust. I had seen and heard about that kind of foolishness too many times. Veronica didn't even realize how she was keeping herself in a situation that could easily turn tragic. She had a cute little girl, too, and I wondered what she was going through at home. Her situation kind of reminded me of mine when I was little. My parents argued all the time and I would sit in my room, crying my butt off. My hands covered my ears to drown out the noise, but it was never enough. I was so glad when my mother left him, and it led to us having a peaceful home. My mother never brought any charges against him, but later in life she told me she regretted that she hadn't. She encouraged me never to put up with an abusive, cheating, or lazy man, and her encouragement was enough for me to know when I was in the wrong kind of relationship. I put my thoughts to the back of my head, and got back to my conversation with Veronica.

"Why don't you just leave him alone, Veronica? There are other men out there, and plenty of men who won't put their hands on you."

"I know. But we've been together for six years and it ain't all that bad. We have our good times, too, and I know when enough is enough. I'll be okay."

There wasn't any thing left to be said. I could talk until I was blue in the face, but Veronica had to wake up in her own time. Hopefully, it wouldn't be too late for her.

I returned to my cubicle, and before I sat down, Claudette came from around the corner with a bright smile on her face. She was always so bubbly, and that kind of fakeness really worked my nerves.

"Good morning," she said, rushing to take off her coat. "It's cold as Alaska out there, isn't it?"

Veronica and I both went over to Claudette's cubicle. Of course, we had to do the morning check, compare what we were wearing. Claudette had on a gray pantsuit too, but to me, the suit looked cheap. She wore a canary yellow shirt underneath and threw in a hint of red to make herself look colorful. Her style in no way worked for me, but I guessed it worked for her, or so she thought. She checked out me and Veronica, and we already knew what was coming next.

"Don't y'all look cute today," she squealed. "Is Liz here yet? I want to take an early lunch and I hope she doesn't mind. I made an appointment to go look at some flowers for my wedding and no other day or time was available."

"I'm sure she wouldn't mind," I said. "Just let her know."

"Let me know what?" Liz said, coming around the corner with a cup of Starbucks Frappuccino in her hand. Now, none of us could come close to the class Liz had. That still didn't stop her from checking me out, and she knew that I too had a style and sexiness about me that couldn't be duplicated. She was a Saks Fifth Avenue kind of woman. I think she may have even had a stylist help her get ready in the morning, because her attire was always so perfect and coordinated with the most exquisite accessories. She was definitely a woman I looked up to and all of us respected her to the fullest.

Claudette followed Liz into her office that was to the left of my cubicle. "I wanted to ask if I could take an early lunch. I'm supposed to meet with a lady who's going to help me pick out flowers for my wedding and I'm running out of time."

"I don't see that being a problem," Liz said, dropping back to her seat. "Just make sure that you get those invoices out to our customers today."

"I'll get started on the rest of them this morning. I mailed out some yesterday, but will make sure the rest are prepared and mailed today. Veronica is double-checking my data entry, and after she unloads her batch, I'll be able to get those out too."

"Sounds good," Liz said. "Chase, will you start getting our invitations together for the Christmas party? I have many executives from the refrigeration company I want to invite, and I'll need to put together some personal invites as well. Come sit in here this morning so we can get started."

I sat in Liz's perfumed office with her for at least two hours, putting together the itinerary for the Christmas party that was three weeks away. Liz asked if I would be bringing anyone with me, and I told her that I wasn't planning to. I was a very private person, and unlike everyone else, I didn't care to bring boyfriends to the workplace and flaunt them. We continued to go over specifics for the party, and when there was a light knock on Liz's door, I turned to see who it was. It was Claudette, and I was surprised to see Korey standing next to her, holding her hand.

"I just wanted to let you know that I'm leaving," she said to Liz. The expression on Korey's face was frozen, and he finally blinked his eyes, looking in another direction.

Liz, of course, invited them into her office.

"How are you, Korey?" she asked. "Congratulations on the engagement. You have Claudette so excited."

"Yeah." He smiled. "We're both pretty excited."

I couldn't tell, especially after all the crap he'd said to me. Claudette looked at me. "Honey, this is Chase Jenkins. She's Liz's secretary and I don't think you met her before. She's only been here for five months, but we love her to death."

I smiled from the bullshit Claudette had said, and stood to extend my hand. "Hi, Korey. Nice meeting you."

He gripped my hand. "You too," he quickly said, then waved his hand in the air. "See you later, Liz. Good seeing you again, but we need to get going so we don't be late."

Liz said good-bye and they left. She was all smiles. "They make such a cute couple," she said. "Remind me so much of my husband and me when we were engaged. I truly hope everything works out for them."

I wanted to choke. I hoped there were no resemblances between her and Claudette, because there was madness stirring behind the scenes. I was so sure

Korey would be calling me tonight, and as handsome as he looked, I had already changed my mind about scratching him from my to-do list. That brotha was *fine*.

Work was long, and awfully busy. Liz kept me on my feet today, and when I got home, I fell back on my bed, so glad to be home. Before I did anything, I went into the bathroom to turn on the shower. I then sat back on my bed, and took my heels off my aching feet. The message light on my phone was blinking, so I tapped the message button to listen. As expected, Drake was calling with his mess. I deleted his messages with a quickness and moved on to the next. There were a few bill collectors calling, particularly one from the student loans that I'd gotten and had never paid back. I had to contact them about deferring my loan, simply because I had no money to pay it. I was already living paycheck to paycheck, and the money I made was in no way enough. I somewhat lived beyond my means, but that consisted of me spending too much money on trying to look good. I had my ponytail done weekly, my nails and toes had to be done, and the money I spent at the M·A·C counter cost me a fortune. Clothes and shoes were high expenses for me, too. I couldn't help that I liked to look good, and my appearance was very important to me. My car payment was almost thirty days late, so I made a mental note to pay it online once I got out of the shower.

My shower was relaxing and long. When I got out, I threw a quick Healthy Choice meal in the microwave, and cut a slice of angel food cake that I had gotten at the grocery store a few days ago. I intended to shut it down early tonight, only because of the lack of sleep I'd gotten the night before. I ate my dinner in no time, and afterward, I turned down the lights in my compact kitchen that was adjacent to my living room. I took a seat on my sectional and turned on the forty-six-inch plasma TV that sat on my black TV stand. It was almost 7:00 P.M., and as *Wheel of Fortune* came to an end, I turned the TV to one of my favorite reality shows. My eyes were slowly fading, but I snapped out of it when the phone rang. The caller ID revealed Korey's cell phone number.

"Can I come see you?" he immediately asked.

"My day was fine, Korey. How was yours?"

"Great. Now, can I come over?"

"Glad that you had a great day. And, what made your day so great?"

"I got a chance to see this chick who's been driving me nuts. She told me that she didn't know who my fiancée was, but I found out today that she lied to me. Why'd you lie to me about not knowing Claudette?"

"I told you that it didn't matter. Obviously, if you want to come see me, the fact that we know each other doesn't matter to you either."

"I want to come see you because I like your style. You seem like a cool person and I want to get to know you better. If you weren't interested, Chase, then it made no sense for you to ask for my number. And if you say that Claudette doesn't matter, then stop playing these games. What's the big deal?"

"The big deal is I'm trying to spare you the grief you may find in the near future. If you think this is going to be one of those slam-bam, thank-you-ma'am deals, you're wrong. I don't mind hooking up with you, but it has to be on my terms. I won't be pressured by a man who is engaged to be married, and if you can play by my rules, I have no problem moving this forward."

"I don't mind playing by your rules, but I can't play by them if you won't even give me your address."

Korey had no idea what he was getting himself into, but I gave him my address so he could come over. I figured it would be a pretty long night, especially since my sexual encounters with Drake had come to an abrupt end. I couldn't believe how horny I was, and I had to get these urges and cravings I had for Korey out of my system. I gave him my address, and before he came, I leaned over to get a quick nap.

When the doorbell rang, I was in a deep sleep. I sat up, squeezing my eyes together while rubbing my hair back with my hand. I wanted to make sure my hair was in place, and as far as I knew, it was. I dropped my silk robe off my shoulders and laid it back on the couch. I stood naked as a jaybird, and very proud of my shapely figure that I worked so hard to get. I made my way to the door.

"Who is it?" I asked.

"Who do you think?" Korey's smart ass answered.

I opened the door, and Korey stood on the other side with his mouth hanging open. Surprisingly, my neighbor across the hall, Lance, was coming up the steps and even he had to take a double . . . triple look. Korey hurried inside, closing the door behind him. He was still in awe, and his eyes were about to fall out of their sockets.

"What . . . Why you—"

I turned, giving him an opportunity to examine my backside. I'm sure it was to his liking. I wasn't in the mood to answer any of his stupid questions, so I quickly cut to the chase.

"Did you bring your condoms?" I asked.

"Yeah, but you gotta be walking around all naked like that?"

I put my hand on my hip. "Grow up, Korey, okay? Haven't you seen a naked woman's body before? You were anxious to come over here for sex, weren't you? And since I have a spark between my legs that needs to be cooled down, I thought we'd have some fun. Get undressed, or would you like me to do that for you as well?"

I couldn't believe he was still standing there in awe. "You're playing, right? As soon as I take off my clothes, you're going to tell me you're playing."

Yet again, he was working my nerves. I walked up to him, and removed his jacket. I tossed it onto the couch, then pulled his muscle-hugging black T-shirt over his head. The look on his face was serious, and he was stunned by my aggressiveness. Once the shirt was gone, I unzipped his jeans and squatted to lower them to his ankles. His package was poked in my direction, and when I stood up, I leaned into his ear. I touched his hardness, massaging it to get his attention.

"Now, does this look anything like I'm playing? Finish up with your shoes and hurry to meet me in my bedroom before I change my mind."

I swayed my hands along Korey's carved chest, and he eased his arm around my waist. He squeezed my nakedness next to his and inched forward for a kiss. I moved my head back to reject it.

"The bedroom," I repeated. "Meet me in the bedroom."

As Korey stepped out of his pants and shoes, I went to my bathroom next to my bedroom and quickly gargled with mouthwash. I had just woken up, so I wanted my breath to be right. Korey wasted no time coming into my bedroom, and I watched as he stood in the doorway, placing a condom on his dick. From what I could see, he was packaged up pretty good. The thickness of his dick made my mouth water, and as it expanded, I was so sure I'd enjoy the next hour or so.

I walked up to Korey, resting my arms on his shoulders. This time, my eyes lowered to his lips, sending him a message that I was now ready for our kiss. He entered my lips tongue first and, as slippery and soft as his lips were, I sure didn't mind. I rubbed the back of his head, and as the kissing became more intense, we backed our way up to the bed. I could feel Korey's hardness poking at my midsection, and that made me more anxious to feel him.

As he held himself up over me, he lowered his head to tease my nipples with the tip of his tongue. They were hard as ever and my tingling had already started. Giving Korey a hint, I widened my legs and placed his hand on the warmth between my legs. His fingers entered me, and with ease, he made several rotations. It wasn't long before his fingers had gotten sticky and I could feel the wetness dripping between my butt cheeks. Korey sucked his fingers while gazing at me with his sexy eyes.

"Can I taste you more?" he politely asked.

"Do you have to ask? I grant you permission to do as you please, so have it your way."

Korey smiled, and dropped his head between my legs. He separated my sticky slit with his fingers and dove in with his curled tongue. My body arched from the vibrations on his mouth and within a few minutes he was tasting the sweetness from my explosive orgasm I had burst into his mouth. It was a good one, too, causing me to claw the sheets and lick the saliva that was dripping from the corners of my mouth. Right behind that followed the entrance of his dick. It tore me wide open and pumped into me with a rhythmic stroke. I was so pleased with the feeling, but so was Korey. His eyes were closed, and when he lifted my legs higher on his shoulders, I gyrated my hips in a circular motion.

"Ahh," he said with relief. "That feels good. Work that pussy, baby. I love a woman who knows how to put herself to work."

My motions had caused Korey to slow down. I knew he was trying to focus so he wouldn't come, but I was anxious to keep the show on the road. I figured a ride from me would send him overboard, so I dropped my legs from his shoulders and turned to lay on my stomach. He kneeled behind me, and with my butt hiked in the air, his hardness entered my slippery hole. The forming juices sounded off in the room, and I gasped for air each time Korey pushed me forward. He had my butts cheeks pulled far apart and his hands gripped them.

"Fuck me harder," I suggested. "Go faster, baby, I want to come again."

"Me too," he said, picking up his pace. His thighs slapped against my backside and I could feel my juices boiling over.

"Ohh, shit," I said, quickly moving back and forth. I couldn't contain myself and cut loose again. He appreciated how wet I was, and it wasn't long before he collapsed behind me. He rolled onto his back, taking deep breaths and touching his chest. "Damn, baby," he said, still out of breath. "You almost gave me a heart attack. That shit was good, and why are you so moist like that? Has it been awhile for you? Because your energy level was extremely high."

"It's been a minute," I said, thinking about the last time Drake and I had sex, which was a little over a month ago. "You did your thing tonight too, and thanks for taking care of that itch for me."

He laughed and looked down at his dripping wet condom. "Anytime," he said, taking it off. "There are plenty of these in my wallet."

I bet there were, and poor Claudette had no idea what her man was doing behind the scenes. I was so sure that I wasn't the first person Korey had been with on the side, and as he lay in bed next to me that night, I asked him if he'd ever cheated on Claudette before.

"Twice," he admitted. "Claudette and I have been together for a long time and I've done something like this two times before. It was with the same person, but I cut it off with her because she wanted to make it more than what it was."

"So, like you and me, it was only a sex thing, right? When you say more, you mean the woman you were creeping with wanted a relationship?"

"Exactly. She knew I was with Claudette and I wasn't trying to end my relationship with her. I just wanted something different, and when she reached out to me about hooking up, I was down with it."

"Just like me, huh? You could've backed away from me, but you didn't. And knowing that Claudette and I work right next to each other, why do you trust me not to say anything to her?"

Korey's arms were around my shoulders and he looked me straight in the eyes. "Honestly, I don't care if you say anything to her. She won't believe you and

I'll deny it. I can almost guarantee you that she'll believe me over you."

I couldn't agree with him more, so there was nothing to dispute. I rested my head on Korey's shoulder, calling it a good night.

Korey got up around 5:00 in the morning, and so did I. Before he left, we tackled another round of sex in the shower and laughed as we lathered and tickled each other's naked bodies. This time, I sat on his lap as he sat on the seat in the shower. My back faced him, and I gave him the ride that I'd failed to give him last night. The water sprayed on our bodies to cool us down, but not by much. I sent him out the door with a true smile on his face, and when I got to work, I couldn't stop reminiscing about the night. Veronica, Claudette, and I sat in the break room eating lunch. When Veronica snapped her fingers in my face, that's when I came out of my trance.

"What did you say?" I asked while nibbling on my sandwich. "Sorry, I was thinking about something."

"What's his name?" Claudette teased. "I know you have a man, Chase, and it's time for you to come clean. Besides, we're going to meet him at the Christmas party, aren't we?"

"As a matter of fact, I was thinking about my father." I wanted to tell her so badly that I was thinking about how tender my pussy felt from fucking her man. As Korey had said, though, she wouldn't believe me. "And as for the Christmas party, no, I'll be attending it alone."

"Well, mostly everyone will have a date and I think you should try to bring someone," Claudette suggested. "You know my boo is coming with me and he is so excited about Christmas this year. We are planning to go on another trip before the wedding, and I'm going to see if Liz will give me a few days off next week."

"Where are the two of you going?" Veronica inquired.

Claudette snapped her fingers and wiggled her neck. "To Vegas," she bragged. "I've never been to Vegas, and you know what they say: what happens in Vegas stays in Vegas. Don't be surprised if we just up and get married."

I doubted that, and Claudette was such a fool. Korey had two sides to him, and I could never understand why a woman could never figure that mess out. As she continued to go on and on about her boo, I bit into my sandwich again, tuning her out. Veronica had done the same. I guess she was just as tired as I was about listening to Claudette ramble on about her so-called perfect relationship with Korey. She loved it when the other people at our job talked about how handsome he was, and mentioned what a cute couple they made. I had made my comments too, and a part of me understood why Claudette was so hooked. Korey was dynamite in bed, and the way he licked between my legs couldn't be forgotten. I got back to thinking about his tongue working its magic, but when my cell phone vibrated, I looked to see who it was. Funny timing, as it was Korey. Claudette had taken a breath from talking to eat her food.

"Yes," I said.

"Can you talk?"

"I have a mouth, don't I?"

He laughed. "You know what I mean. Is Claudette near you?"

I looked right at her. "Nope. And for a man who doesn't seem to care either way, why are you asking?"

"I just want to be sure. You know I don't want to go around breaking any hearts," he joked.

"Oh, I understand. So, what's up?"

"Are you thinking about me?"

"Maybe."

"Well, I'm thinking about you. Can I come over tonight, or would you prefer that we go out to dinner tonight? It's Friday and I know you ain't staying cooped up in your apartment."

Claudette had mentioned earlier that they were going to the movies. I guess he was willing to cancel their plans. "You don't have any other plans? I thought you did."

"Plans to be with you. Are you game or what?"

"Not tonight," I whispered. Claudette and Veronica were taking in every word I'd said. They were some nosy-ass bitches, I swear. "Maybe next week."

"You got plans with somebody else tonight?"

I disliked Korey's insecurities and they really had no place in the kind of relationship we were beginning to have. "His name is Drake. Like you, I have something on the side and we have to be patient with each other's circumstances. Next week, I promise."

"Fuck Drake. I want to see you tonight. Put that fool on the calendar for next week, not me."

"Good-bye, playboy, this is really a bad time. Elephant ears are around me, so call me later."

"No, I'll see you later. If you slam the door in my face, too bad."

I shut my phone and looked at Veronica and Claudette. Their eyes were bugged and lips were pursed.

"I told you she be lying," Veronica said. "And, yes, these elephant ears were listening. Who is Drake?"

"None of your business," I said. "He's not worth me discussing and neither is that phone call."

"Sounds like you got yourself a stalker," Claudette laughed.

That's right, trick, and he just happens to be your man, I thought. *Korey had better not show up tonight.* And if he did, well, all I was going to do was . . . put him to good use.

Chapter 3

After another month of dealing with Korey, I could feel things getting out of hand. He had been at my place at least four days out of every week, and it was hard to get him to leave. His cell phone rang off the hook, and when I'd ask who it was, he always told me it was Claudette. Even her attitude at work had changed, simply because that trip she was supposed to take to Vegas had already been canceled and put on the backburner. She wasn't happy about that at all, but was still making plans for her wedding that was due to take place in March.

According to Korey, he had considered changing his mind. I made it clear not to do it because of me, and he assured me that his decision was not based on that alone. The truth was now coming to the light, and let him tell it, Claudette was a spoiled brat who his mother simply adored. She and Claudette were close, and as a matter of fact, his mother was the one who had introduced the two of them. Yes, he admitted to

still loving her, but also said that he was in no way
ready for marriage. That was obvious.

I was a bit annoyed that he wasn't playing by my
rules as he'd promised, but for the last couple of days,
I told him not to come over. He showed up anyway,
and I switched to Plan B for men who didn't know
how to listen. I let him stay outside in the rain, beg-
ging to come in. When he left, I sent him a text, reminding him that I meant what I'd said. The only way
that we were going to continue as we had been would
be if Korey listened to me. If I didn't want to be bothered with him, then so be it. He was so worried about
me giving the goods to someone else, and even though
I was in no way saving myself for him, I didn't like giving myself to two men at once. I knew I was wasting
my time with Korey, but for now, it was fun to watch
what was transpiring around me.

Claudette's perkiness had calmed down, and I listened to her daily phone calls where she whispered to
Korey, asking if everything was okay. Like many
women, she knew when something was going on with
her man, but she was in denial. She was determined to
have her little perfect world through marriage, but little did she know, that kind of world did not exist.

The Christmas party was tonight and I had gone out
of my way to make sure everything was perfect as Liz
had asked. She wanted gold accessories to match the
red and green linen tablecloths, excluding silver alto-
gether. Numerous dozens of poinsettias were bought
in to liven up the ballroom, and special gifts had been
wrapped for each employee and placed underneath a
sixteen-inch Christmas tree. As for the food, the main

course was steak or salmon. I was able to sample the food, just to make sure it would be to Liz's satisfaction. To me, it was. Some very important executives were attending with their spouses, and the administrative staff was invited as well. I figured that it wouldn't be a good idea for me to go alone, and maybe Veronica and Claudette were right. I would look stupid without a date, and as much as I wanted to call Drake and see if he'd go with me, I couldn't. I had washed my hands of him and he had gotten the picture. His phone calls came to an abrupt end, and I figured he had moved on with the chick with long legs.

With that in mind, I stopped my neighbor Lance as he was entering his apartment last week, and asked if he would attend the party with me. He was stunned that I'd asked him, but in return, I had to go to his Christmas party with him. We had gone to his Christmas party last night, and I was surprised by how much fun we'd had. By all means, Lance was no head turner, but he was genuinely a nice guy. His coworkers thought so as well, and they couldn't stop bragging about how helpful he had been to them at the office. He was the info systems person, and it seemed as if everyone liked him. He had a great sense of humor, too, and he opened up to me about the numerous ladies I'd seen come to his apartment. They were all friends, he said, and that's how he intended to keep it. He questioned me about standing naked in the doorway that day, and I laughed, explaining to him how anxious I was for the man at the door. If anything, Lance and I could become good friends. I was in no way attracted to him sexually, but I wasn't sure if he felt the same.

For the Christmas party, I wore a black and red

strapless silk dress that boosted up my cleavage and squeezed my perfect waistline. My backside looked even plumper. Every man I had dated talked about how soft my butt was to grip. I kept my hair in a pony-tail, but added bangs that swooped on my forehead. My hazel eyes were even prettier with the long eye-lashes I'd had put on and my lips were glossed with M•A•C. Giving me a bit more height, I stepped in my two-tone black and red heels, feeling as if I looked dy-namite as ever. I tucked my purse underneath my arm, and went to Lance's door to knock. He wore the same black suit that he'd had on last night, and even though it was repeated attire, he still looked nice. A pressed white shirt was underneath and a thin black tie was around his neck. His bald head was cleanly shaven, and I loved that he wore a goatee.

"You look amazing," he said, kissing my cheek. "Are you driving, or shall I?"

"Thanks for the compliment and you look nice too. You can drive," I said, tossing him my keys. "But drive my car."

"Why?" he said as we made our way down the steps. " 'Cause you have issues with my truck?"

"Let's just say that I have a destination to reach tonight. We may not have time to ask anybody for a jump."

Lance cracked up, and that's what I appreciated about him. He wasn't a smart ass, and could always find humor in anything I said. He opened the car door for me, and after I got in, he did.

"So, what kind of behavior should I be on tonight? Are the people you work with uptight or loose? Can I crack a joke and expect to get laughs or stares after-ward?"

"That depends on what kind of joke you tell. As for the people, you'll get a mixture of both. Just don't be over friendly, and do not tell anyone that we're neighbors."

"Am I supposed to be your boyfriend, or just a friend?"

"Just a friend. A good friend and you've known me for years."

Lance nodded and sped off to the hotel where the Christmas party was.

When we arrived at the Four Seasons hotel, the ballroom was already packed. I was supposed to arrive early, just to make sure everything was in order, but so much for that. The room was dimly lit by the numerous chandeliers that hung from the ceiling. The tables were covered with red velvet tablecloths and decorated with gold and white plating. The serving tables were covered with green tablecloths and an array of foods was offered. Champagne and glasses were on another table, and an open bar was available for those who wanted to drink. The DJ was kicking up light jazz, but with the loud talking that filled the room, the music was drowned out.

The first person I spotted was Liz. She looked magnificent, as she stood conversing with four white women. Her red, long dress was like a silhouette of her perfect, slim, model-like body. Her curves were in the right places, and she portrayed nothing but class. I assumed that the black man next to her was her husband. She hadn't lied; they were a good-looking couple. His suit had to be tailored, and the way it clung to his frame said so. I staggered back a bit because of how fine he was, and I hoped that my date didn't notice. Liz's husband looked to be in his early fifties, and the tint of gray in his hair and beard made him even sexier. Now, I wasn't a big fan of men with gray in their hair, but when it came in that fashion, I had to give the man props. The smell of money was on both of them, and I was glad to see them strongly representing the black folks in the room. The same, of course, could not be said for Veronica and her date. She was blooming in her flowers again, this time red and white. Her date had the nerve to be in a lime green suit, and when I saw the pimp hat on the table, I could have puked. Without even seeing his shoes, I could already imagine them. I didn't see Claudette and Korey yet, so I walked over to our table and introduced Veronica and her pimp daddy to Lance.

Veronica extended her hand to Lance. "Hi," she said. "Nice meeting you."

"Same here," Lance said. Pimp daddy never extended his hand; all he did was toss his head back and say, "What up."

Lance and I took our seats, and I immediately asked Veronica if she'd seen Claudette.

"Not yet." She looked behind me. "Oh, here she comes. She just came in."

I turned and almost fell over in my seat. This bitch had on the same dress as me, only hers had straps on it and she wore a silk shawl on her shoulders. I had shown the dress to her in an apparel magazine that we looked through, and she knew darn well that I had mentioned buying the dress. I could have ripped that sucker off of her, but I smiled, pretending as if it were all good. Besides, Korey looked spectacular in his black suit, and thinking about what would go down with us tonight put me somewhat at ease. He was too handsome to be by Claudette's side, and when she skidded our way with flats on, I wanted to laugh my butt off. She didn't even have the right taste to jazz up the dress like I had.

"Hello, ladies," she said, kissing the air beside our cheeks. She looked at me and pursed her juicy, soup cooler lips. "You look nice. And, so do I," she joked.

I couldn't even respond, but I made a mental note to spill some wine on her dress tonight. She turned to Korey and proudly made her introduction. "I know some of you met my fiancé, Korey, before, but here he is again."

Lance's eyes widened, and I suspected that he remembered Korey from my apartment that night. Either way, we all spoke and everyone got seated. That included Liz and her husband as well, as dinner was starting to be served.

Liz pulled out her compact mirror and wiped the minimal sweat from her forehead. She sucked her pearly white teeth, then turned to her husband. "Is there any lipstick on my teeth? I'd hate to be talking to all of these people with lipstick on my teeth."

Her husband examined her teeth, telling her that there wasn't. She closed her compact, and looked across the table, checking us out as well. "You ladies are hooked up tonight," she laughed. "We have to make sure that we take plenty of pictures. Chase, did you bring your camera?"

I wasn't no darn photographer, and I hadn't anticipated running around here taking pictures. This was a time to enjoy my evening too, and I had hoped Liz wasn't expecting me to do any work. "No, Liz, I forgot to bring one."

She dug in her purse and passed her camera across

the table. "Here, sweetie. Take as many as you can. No big deal, just whenever you feel like it."

"Sure," I said, picking up the camera. I told Lance to smile, and when he did, I flashed a picture of him. When I turned to my left, I lifted the camera to take a picture of Korey and Claudette. She was all smiles, but he wasn't. He had a cold look in his eyes, but I took the picture anyway, cutting Claudette out of it. I snapped a picture of pimp daddy and Veronica, then took one of Liz and her husband. I made a mental note: I'd have to cut her out of the picture, and keep a picture of him for myself.

Lance was two steps ahead of me, and when he suggested a group picture, I gave the camera to him. We all gathered close, and I squeezed in right next to Korey. I looked at it as an opportunity to squeeze his butt, and when he put his arm around my waist, that's what I did. He softly touched the side of my hip and smiled. Lance took the picture and we all took our seats again. Moments later, the waiters came over to the table to serve our salads and bread. They filled our glasses with water, and asked if anyone preferred iced tea. Liz did, and Claudette followed suit.

"I'll take a glass too," she said, turning to Korey. "Honey, do you want some tea, or would you prefer to get something at the bar?"

"It doesn't matter," he said in a griping tone. "I guess I'll get something later."

I knew what his gripes were about, and as much as he was eyeballing Lance, it was obvious. Lance seemed to pick up on the stares too, and I noticed him looking a bit uncomfortable. As we all talked and ate our salads, pimp daddy started bringing attention to himself. He frowned while looking at the salad. He kept picking through it and letting out deep sighs.

"Where's the salad dressin' at?" he said. "Why this doggone thing ain't got no salad dressin' on it?"

Veronica was already embarrassed by him, I could tell. "It's a Caesar salad, Tony. They don't come with a lot of dressing."

"I can't eat this mess. As much money as this hotel got, you would think they wouldn't be so skimpy with the salad dressin'."

"Well, don't eat it," she said. "Eat the bread."

He picked up a piece of bread, then dropped it back into the decorated Christmas basket. "Feel how hard that bread is. It feels like a brick. I know you may not have a problem eatin' that mess, but I sure as hell won't eat it."

Veronica looked around the table, noticing everybody's eyes on them. Yes, we tried to play it off by continuing to eat, but Tony was being rude and obnoxious. I hoped she had a Plan B for the night, and it was evident that she'd need one. Maybe if I had a greasy pork chop or doggie bone, I would have thrown it to Tony to keep him quiet. He knew better, and this wasn't the time or place to be complaining. The food and drinks were free, so he should have dealt with it. He could stop for a happy box at Fried Rice Kitchen on his way home.

I was so touched when Lance stopped the waiter and asked if he could have a side cup of dressing. When the waiter came back with it, Lance passed it over to Tony, just to keep down confusion. He waved Lance off.

"Nah, that's okay, bruh. I'm good," he said, wiping

his hands with the napkin. "They can have this shit. I'm going to get me somethin' to drink."

He got up from the table, and, as expected, those lime green Stacy Adamses matched his suit to a tee. Veronica kept her head low, and I felt embarrassed for her. She should have known better than to bring a rat like that one to this kind of an event.

"So," Liz said, dabbing her mouth with a napkin, "Korey, are you prepared for the big day? Two months before our wedding, Steven and I were getting pretty anxious and we had even thought about squashing the wedding and going to Vegas."

Claudette laughed and clenched Korey's hand. "How ironic! We thought about that too, but Korey and his dad had to go on a business trip that weekend. I'm glad we didn't do it, though, and we are so looking forward to our wedding."

I thought Liz was talking to Korey, but Claudette always had to speak for him. That was a no-no for any man, and a for-real man didn't need any woman to speak for him. Korey just smiled and sipped his water. I couldn't help but throw in my two cents. "So, when is the wedding again? I know you've told us at least a million times, but you have yet to mention anything about us getting invitations."

Claudette threw her hand back. "Girl, you know I got y'all. You will definitely be invited and I may even let you see my dress before the wedding."

Liz started talking about her wedding day and everyone, including her fine-ass husband, was tuned in. Now, I wasn't into older men, but damn! Why did he have that Denzel Washington swagga going on? Whenever he talked, his lips looked so juicy and sexy. I thought about them being pressed against my pussy, and when I blinked away, it was as if Korey had been reading my mind. I wished that he would stop staring at me, because if anyone had been paying attention like I was, they would have suspected something. Good thing Lance had excused himself to go to the restroom.

Veronica's date, Tony, came back and sat with two drinks in his hand. Veronica reached for one of the glasses.

"Get your own damn glass," he snapped. He sipped from one glass, then let out a belch that echoed in the room. If that weren't enough, he didn't even excuse himself. I kept thinking, *Handle your business, girl, please handle your business. Now!*

"Excuse you," Veronica snapped.

He pointed to himself. "Excuse who? Me?"

"Yes, Tony. You belched out loud and everyone heard it."

He frowned and acted as if she was talking down to him. "I don't give a damn," he said. "I belched, so what? You belch at home and I don't hear you excusin' yourself. Why put on a front now?"

Veronica dropped her napkin on the table and stood up. "Come on, Tony. Let's go home. I knew this was going to be a bad idea, and you couldn't go one day without complaining about something."

He cocked his head back. "Sit your fat ass down," he said.

By then, my hand was over my mouth, Liz's eyes were bugged, and Korey and Steven looked disgusted. Claudette looked as if she wanted to bust out laughing, but I'd give that bitch something to laugh about later.

"Maybe you all should leave," Steven suggested.

"This is the wrong place and time for that, man, and you shouldn't be talking to your lady like that."

I knew Steven was my kind of man. *Go ahead, baby, speak up.* Lance came back over to the table, trying to see what was going on. It didn't take long for him to see.

Veronica was near tears, and Tony's eyes cut Steven like a knife. "Mind your own business, fool. I can't stand to be around salad-eatin', uppity black folks who forget where the fuck they come from. Enjoy the white man's meal, and I'm sure they'll be kickin' up the music in a few minutes so you all can snap your fingers and do the jig. Stupid shit," he said, looking at Veronica. "Are you goin' home with me or not? If not, you'd better find a ride home because I'm takin' the car."

I was hyped about what Veronica was going to say next, but she had an unsure look on her face. Steven stood up from the table, and Lance grabbed Veronica's arm. "Chase and I will take you home," he said. "You don't need to go anywhere with him, and I don't need to tell you why."

Everyone waited for Veronica to make a move, but I sat back and said not one word. I could almost predict the outcome, and when she got her purse, I could have gotten up and punched her myself.

"I have to go pick up my daughter from the baby-sitter's. I apologize for this and I'll see everyone on Monday."

She looked downright humiliated, but what could anyone at the table do? We all shook our heads and watched as Tony and Veronica left together, arguing on their way out the door. Claudette couldn't wait to open her mouth.

"That is such a shame. I had no idea Tony was that kind of person, and I feel so sorry for Veronica."

Liz quickly spoke up. "Listen, we're not going to sit here and talk about what just happened. Let's enjoy the night, and I will speak to Veronica on Monday."

"A woman like her can't be reasoned with," Steven added. "Sometimes, something tragic has to happen before they even wake up."

Liz looked at her husband and snapped, "I said, let's not discuss this. It has no place at this table and I mean what I said."

I wasn't shocked when he snapped back, because he looked like the kind of man who didn't take no shit. Those were the ones I admired. "I'll say whatever I wish to say. Watch your tone, woman, and let's do enjoy our evening."

What the fuck! I guess everything that looks good on the outside isn't. They seemed as if they had some drama too, and this was another reason why I would never, ever bring a for-real date to a company event. Liz cut her eyes at her husband, and throughout dinner, our table remained pretty quiet. I made small talk with Lance, and Claudette was trying to make conversation with Korey. He was in no way listening to her, and when I got up to get something to drink, he got up as well.

"Do you want something to drink?" he asked Claudette.

"A soda will be fine. Thanks, honey."

I stood in the long line, waiting to get a drink. Korey stood behind me, doing his best not to look obvious.

"What's up with the dude you're with? Isn't he your neighbor?"

"Yes." I smiled and waved at a coworker from another department. "Why?"

He whispered, "Are you fucking him too?"

"That's none of your business. How many times do I have to tell you to stay out of my business? I thought we had an understanding, and if we don't, then we need to end this."

Korey couldn't say another word, because Claudette was making her way over to us. "We'll talk later," he whispered, and smiled at Claudette when he turned his head.

"This line is too long," she said. "My water is fine. Why don't you come back to the table to finish your food? Afterward, I want to dance." She wiggled her shoulders, looking silly as ever.

"That's fine," he said. "I'll get something to drink later."

They walked away, and I continued to wait in line. As I got closer to the bar, Lance approached me.

"Risky, risky, risky," he said, playfully wiping his forehead. "You are a risk taker, aren't you?"

"What are you talking about?" I smiled.

"You know exactly what I'm talking about. He's the brotha who was at your apartment that day, isn't he?"

I placed my finger on my lip. "Shh, don't talk so loud. And, no, it isn't."

"You're not a good liar. Besides, you can't dispute something I saw with my own eyes. He can't keep his eyes off of you tonight, and, as a man, I know what it's like to have two women in the room who you're—"

I placed my hand over Lance's mouth. "Okay, you're

right. Now, can we talk about this in the car or at home?"

He laughed, and as we stood in line talking about other things, Korey was making a spectacle of himself. If Claudette wasn't paying attention to him, then she was crazy. I guess she thought she had him wrapped around her finger, but that was in no way the case.

Lance and I got our drinks, and, after dinner, everyone started dancing. I was really having a good time, and so was Lance. I even got a chance to dance with Liz's husband, Steven, and as he turned me in circles, not only was my head spinning, but so were my thoughts. I liked Liz a lot, but I was starting to like her husband so much more. I added him to my to-do list and was serious about somehow luring him to my bedroom

As he and I wrapped up our dance, I looked by the doorway and saw Korey standing by the door. He nudged his head toward the exit, and walked out the door. Claudette and some of our other coworkers were sitting at the table talking to Lance. I told him I needed to go to the restroom and would be right back.

As I exited the ballroom, I looked down the huge hallway, but didn't see Korey. I then noticed a cracked door, and his hand waving out of it from inside. I swiped my sweaty bangs away from my forehead, making my way toward the room. When I got to the door, Korey pulled me inside. The room was pitch black and I couldn't see a thing.

"What do you want?" I whispered. "I'm serious about calling you later, and I promise you that I will."

"I can't wait until later. You've put me off long enough, and I have a feeling that you'll be over at your neighbor's house tonight."

I didn't even bother to tell Korey that he was so wrong about me and Lance. Instead, I flipped the lights on by the door, noticing nothing but a marble floor and tall black curtains that separated one section of the party room from another. I hit the lights again, and directed Korey behind one of the curtains, just in case someone came in. When we got behind the curtain, I hiked up my dress and took Korey's hand. I eased it into my panties, letting his fingers go to work.

"Is that what you want?" I asked, resting my arms on his shoulders.

"Yes." He sighed from relief while feeling my insides. "You're damn right that's what I want."

I backed away from Korey's touch and sat on the floor. I knew we didn't have much time, so there was no need to get completely undressed. I moved the crotch of my silk panties aside, feeling just how wet they already were. Korey didn't want to put his dick inside of me. Instead, he held my panties aside for me and used his tongue for immediate pleasure. He got a kick out of tasting me, but not as much as I did. I leaned back on my elbows, dropping my head back from the spectacular performance. Korey was jabbing his fingers and tongue at the same time, trying to squeeze every ounce of juice out of me. It wasn't long before he got what he wanted, and I fell flat on my back, taking deep breaths.

"Ohh, Korey," I moaned. "Nobody ever sucked my pussy this well. You are so good at that, but please put your dick in me. Send me back out there with a glowing smile on my face."

"You bet I will," he confirmed, and put on a condom. He liked to hit it from the back, so when I turned on my stomach, and separated my legs, he quickly went in. His hands roamed all over my butt, and as he soaked my insides from behind, he excited me even more when he used his finger to tease my anal hole. He managed to sink his finger inside, and I let out a gasping sound that caught me off guard.

"Can I put my dick in there?" he whispered. "Trust me, baby, it will feel so, so good."

I didn't gesture either way, but no response from me gave him the go-ahead. Korey pulled out of one hole, and carefully eased into the other. I was tense as ever, but his slow pace put me at ease. His fingers dipped into my wetness, and with all of the multitasking going on, my body was trembling all over. I couldn't back it up like I wanted to, but Korey was busy doing his thing.

"Do you like that?" he asked while sliding himself in and out of me. He started traveling from one hole to the other, skillfully doing so and causing me minimal pain. I guess the fact that I was sopping wet helped, and as we both got ready to climax together, he stayed in my vagina.

"Yes, I love it," I confirmed. "But hurry. I know *some* people may be wondering where we are."

"Fuck them," he groaned. "Let them wonder. To hell with your neighbor, too. I bet that he don't make you feel like this, does he?"

Korey had the right rhythm, and, yes, he knew how to turn up the heat in order for me to say what he wanted. "Hell, no, my neighbor can't fuck me like this! Only you can do it, baby, only you."

"Only you too," he shot back, squeezing his butt and letting his excitement seep into the condom. He lay on my back for a minute, allowing himself to regroup. He then moved my ponytail aside, and pecked down my neck. "Just a quick FYI," he said. "I'm not going to marry Claudette. This pussy is too good for me to let go and it would be so stupid for me to marry her. I'll be making the biggest mistake of my life. I know how you feel about us having a relationship, but think about it, okay? The way we connect can't be ignored, and even you, yourself, can't deny your feelings for me."

It was the wrong time for me to elaborate on what Korey had said, so I didn't. I just told him that we'd talk later and left it at that. Truth was, I didn't want a relationship with Korey. All I wanted to do was fuck him and keep him at a distance. Now, I understood how he felt about not marrying Claudette, as that would definitely be a stupid move on his part. But if he ever thought our relationship would go any further than what it was, he was sadly mistaken. In no way did I trust men to the level where I would ever seek a relationship with him so quickly. Especially after he'd shown me how easy it was for him to deceive Claudette. Korey was coldhearted and had little or no regret for what he was doing. He had proven himself to be a complete dog, and there wasn't a chance in hell I would ever run around and call someone like him my man.

We quickly straightened our clothes, and I left the room first. I went to the bathroom to tidy myself up a bit, but had no makeup in my purse to freshen up. My dress had a few wrinkles too, but that could be attributed to dancing so much. I had to live with my appearance, and when I returned to the table, the only people who were there were Lance, Claudette, and Korey. Liz was off running her mouth again, and so was her husband. I dropped to my seat, immediately taking a sip of water to calm myself.

"I thought you got lost," Lance said. "Two of your coworkers came over here looking for you, but I told them you'd gone to the ladies' room."

"I did, but I also walked around the hotel to check it out. It's a beautiful place and you should go see it for yourself."

Lance just gazed at me and let out a soft snicker.

"What?" I said. "What's so funny?"

"Nothing. Nothing at all."

We sat quietly for a few minutes, watching other people dance. I did my best to ignore Korey, but it was so darn hard to. He was facing Claudette, and every time he looked over her shoulder, there I was. I noticed something white on his lightly trimmed mustache, unsure if it was the creamy sauce from dinner or from me. I pointed to the spot on my lip, trying to get his attention. He caught on quickly and licked his lips from side to side.

"What are you doing?" Claudette said to Korey, then turned to look behind her. I was already looking in another direction.

"I was trying to get something off my lips. Is there anything there?"

She picked up a napkin and dabbed his lips. "Looks like something clear and sticky, probably the sauce from the fettuccini. Either way," she said, pecking his lips, "I got it."

I had to turn my head before I burst out laughing. When I did, all Lance could do was shake his head. He knew exactly what had happened that night, and when we got in the car, he couldn't stop talking about how obvious Korey and I really were.

"I mean, if Claudette had been really paying attention to her man," Lance said, "she would have known that he was interested in you."

"I regret that his looks were so obvious, and I hope you're not upset with me, are you?"

Lance broke it down to me gently. "You're not my woman, and I have played that game many, many times before. So in no way am I mad at you."

I took a deep breath, wondering if Claudette really suspected that anything was going on between Korey and me, or if she was simply naïve.

Chapter 4

On Monday, Veronica called in sick. I had an idea why, and since Liz called in and said she wouldn't be in until afternoon, I decided to take matters into my own hands. I wanted to find out where Veronica lived. The more I thought about it, Tony really irked the hell out of me. If what I thought was going on, that fool was going to pay.

Claudette wasn't in yet, so I crept into Liz's office, closing the door behind me. I started looking through her important files, and when I found the one with Veronica's name on it, I opened it up. The first thing I saw was her salary. It showed that she made $46,300 a year, and that was a bit much for someone who basically did nothing but enter data into a computer, check it, print it off, and mail it. My job was much harder than hers and Claudette's both. I swear, secretaries always got screwed, but did more than anyone. I quickly wrote down her address, then placed her file back into the drawer. Just for the hell of it, I looked for

Claudette's file and found it too. When I looked at her salary, I couldn't believe my eyes. She made $51,000 a year, and was in no way worth that kind of money. I jotted down her address too. Since she had been calling Korey so much while he was at my apartment, I already had her phone number. I put her file back into the drawer, and continued to be nosy. I was looking for anything that gave me some information about Liz's husband. He called the office sometimes looking for her, and had I known he was hooked up like that, I would have made my move on him, instead of Korey. I couldn't find anything until I flipped through Liz's business card holder. His business card was in there, showing that he was a director of financial advisors. Sounded pretty important to me, and maybe it was time for me to get my finances in order.

When I came out of Liz's office, I heard sniffles coming from Claudette's cubicle. I walked over to it, noticing her with Kleenex in her hand and dabbing her eyes. I guessed Korey had finally broken the news to her, and it was quite a sight to see Claudette's face beet red.

I pretended to be so concerned. "What's wrong, Claudette? Are you okay?"

Giving her attention made her cry even louder. I rubbed her back while pursing my lips. I was sure all Korey had to do was give it to her like he had given it to me at the Christmas party, and she'd be fine. That shit he did to me at the party was off the chain, and I hadn't forgotten about it since. There was no way Claudette could hang with something like him, and it was obvious that he was getting all of his pleasures from me.

"I'm okay," she said, starting to calm herself. "I . . . I just lost him, that's all. I loved him so much and I lost him."

"Men will come and go, sweetie. You're a beautiful person, Claudette, and Korey can always be replaced."

She snapped her head to the side, quickly correcting me. "No, it's not Korey I'm talking about. It's my cat, Bubbles. He died yesterday and I am so, so miserable."

I stood with a blank expression on my face, and had a visualization of me smacking her upside her head. This bitch was all choked up over a cat? What kind of shit was that? I really didn't know what else to say to her. As a matter of fact, I didn't say anything else. I left her cubicle, shaking my head. She and Korey were complete opposites, and I knew he wasn't up to baby-sitting this kind of so-called woman for the rest of his life.

Liz had already put a few things on my desk for me to do, so I got busy. She didn't show up until almost noon, so I pushed my lunch back by an hour.

Before going into her office, she stood by my cubicle with three shopping bags in her hand. I thought she'd told me that she had an early morning business meeting to attend, but I had no idea that Saks Fifth Avenue was conducting corporate meetings. Some people could get away with all kind of shit, but I guess that's just how things are.

"Did Veronica call in sick today?" she asked.

"Yes. She said she'd be in on Wednesday and wanted to take a couple of days off because she wasn't feeling well."

"I'm so worried about her. I couldn't sleep that night, and even though I don't want to be critical of anyone's man, she can definitely do better. Your boyfriend,

Lance, was a nice guy, too. I got a chance to speak to him and he really likes you a lot."

I wanted to tell her what I thought of her husband, but I kept my mouth shut. "Lance is a good friend of mine. There's nothing serious going on between us, but he is one of the nicest men I've ever met."

"Well, don't let him slip away. He's—"

Liz paused when she saw Claudette enter her cubicle with about two dozen pretty pink roses.

"Oh, those are so, so pretty. I guess I don't have to ask who gave them to you."

Claudette was all smiles. I peered over her cubicle to look at the flowers and they were, indeed, beautiful. Costly, too.

"Bubbles died yesterday and I've been sick to my stomach. Korey sent these flowers today, just to cheer me up."

Oh, no, he didn't, I thought. What was that shit all about? He knew those flowers would irritate me and they did. Claudette even read the card to us:

So sorry for your loss, but I hope these flowers brighten your day. I love you, wifey, and I'll see you tonight.

Liz was grinning just as hard as Claudette was. "Both of you are so lucky to have decent men in your lives. I wish Veronica would come to her senses. I've thought about getting her some help." She looked at me. "Chase, see if you can get her on the phone for me. Hold all of my calls for about two hours, and once you get her on the phone, go ahead and take your lunch."

I called Veronica's phone, but no one answered. I buzzed into Liz's office to tell her, since her door was closed. "All right," she said. "Go take your lunch and try her again when you get back."

I told Liz that I would and got ready to go to lunch. Claudette wanted to know where I was going, but I didn't feel like sitting at a table yakking with her. Besides, I had a phone call to make. Korey's ass was in hot water for those flowers.

"I have to meet my cousin to drop off some money to her," I said to Claudette. "We'll do lunch tomorrow. Do you want me to stop and get you something?"

"No, I'll just grab something quick from the lunchroom. Or, I just may call Korey to see if he'll have lunch with me."

I hoped she didn't see me roll my eyes. All this chick knew was Korey this, Korey that. Korey, Korey, Korey, my ass! "Okay, Claudette. See you when I get back."

I left, and as soon as I reached the lobby, I was already dialing my cell phone. Korey didn't answer, but when I got off the elevator, my phone rang. It was him.

"What's up, baby?" he said. "I know you ain't trying to get at me in the middle of the day. What did I do to deserve this?"

"Don't baby me, Korey. What's up with the flowers?"

"What flowers?"

"The pink flowers you sent Claudette today."

"What? I didn't send her any flowers."

"Quit lying."

"Seriously, I didn't. If she got some flowers, she must have gotten them from someone else."

"Yeah, right. Do you expect me to believe that? You know darn well you felt bad because of her stupid cat. Of course you thought the flowers would make your precious wifey feel better."

"I didn't send those flowers, but now that you mention it, I know who did. My mother did, because she felt bad about Bubbles. I liked Bubbles too, and I understand how Claudette feels. But those flowers I had nothing to do with."

"I don't believe you, but that's cool. Go ahead and do you."

"Are you jealous?" He chuckled. "I know you ain't jealous over no stupid flowers, are you? And if I did buy them, what's wrong with a man trying to cheer up his woman? I'm not as coldhearted as you think I am."

"Well, I am. And since you think this shit is so funny, I have a suggestion for you. Keep cheering up your woman, and I'll see the two of you at the wedding."

I hung up, and Korey kept trying to call back. I refused to answer, and finally turned off my phone. I ran a few errands, then headed back to work.

The afternoon moved by slowly. I never could get in touch with Veronica, and Liz had given up. She seemed extremely quiet today, and when I asked if she was okay, she told me that the situation with Veronica really bothered her. It troubled me too, but I wasn't going to sit around feeling sorry for Veronica. I was going to help her . . . in my own way, of course.

When five o'clock came around, I was out. Claudette and I took the elevator to the parking garage, and, yet again, she loved the attention she got from the ladies who adored her roses.

"Someone must really love you," one lady said. "Those are beautiful."

"They're from my fiancé, Korey, and, yes, he does love me. A lot."

She was working me so badly, and I couldn't wait to get off the elevator so I could run to my car to get away from her. Without saying "I'll see you tomorrow," I hurried to my car and turned my cell phone back on. It showed that I had ten voice mail messages, but I listened to not one. I knew they were from Korey, so I deleted them. He was on my shit list now, and that was a place he definitely didn't want to be.

I drove down the curvy street, looking for Veronica's address. I finally saw her house, and was really surprised by how small it was. It was a ranch-style house with two small windows on the front. A one-car garage was attached, and parked in the driveway was a raggedy old car, sitting up with bricks underneath it. Oil stained the driveway, and trash particles were all over the grass. The house was supposed to be painted white, but it almost looked gray. When I got to the door, it was filthy as ever. Dirty fingerprints were all over it, and I could only imagine what the inside looked like. Veronica made enough money to live better than this, but maybe her money was being spent on the wrong things, or on the wrong person.

I rang the doorbell several times, but no one answered. I heard movement inside, though, and when a little girl asked who I was, I asked if Veronica was at home.

"No, she's not here," she yelled through the door.

"Is your father home?"

"He doesn't live here."

"I'm sorry to bother you, but are you alone? I know your mother probably told you not to speak to strangers, but I think your mother may be in some trouble."

The girl didn't answer, but Veronica did. She opened the door, but wouldn't let me inside. Immediately, I noticed a bruise on the side of her face. Makeup couldn't cover that up; no wonder she wanted to take two days off.

"What is it, Chase? You shouldn't have come here."

"Maybe I shouldn't have, but I was worried about you. Everyone is, and I've been calling your phone all day."

"I know. I didn't feel like talking to anyone. I appreciate your concern, but I'll be okay."

For whatever reason, I couldn't accept that. Maybe I was out of line for coming here, but I couldn't walk away. "Can I come inside and talk to you for a few minutes, please? I won't be long."

Veronica opened the door wider and let me inside. She invited me to sit on the couch, but it was so nasty that I started to decline. The smell inside was horrible, and I could tell the trash hadn't been taken out. She told her daughter to go into her room, and she left the living room while Veronica and I talked.

"Look," I said, "I don't know where to begin, but maybe I should start with some things that you don't know about me. I grew up in an abusive home and I watched my mother and father go at it all the time. I hated my father, and there are not too many people I'm willing to admit this to, but he also molested me. When I told my mother, that was her wake-up call. She did the right thing, and removed both of us from a horrific situation. For years, we kept what had happened to me a secret, but what my father did to me has affected my life in so many ways.

"When I saw Tony the other day, I saw my father. The way he talked to you is the way my mother was treated. A controlling man will do anything, and I'm not accusing him of doing anything to your daughter, but I hope that's not the case. You can do so much better, Veronica, but, first, you need to realize what a beautiful person you really are."

She looked down at the floor, already starting to

wipe her tears. "I know," she said. "But I love him so much, Chase. He is so good to me, and you don't know all that he does for me. I mean, we have our problems, but we always work through them. No relationship is perfect and I don't expect mine to ever be that way."

"Perfect, no. Respectful, yes. If he respected you, he wouldn't put his hands on you. If he does so much for you, no offense, but you wouldn't be living like this. How can you not see that, Veronica? You are in denial, and he has brainwashed you into believing that you really need him. You don't, and if you walk away from this, you will feel so much better about life and everything. I see the sadness in your eyes and that is something you can't hide."

Veronica sat silent for a while, then spoke up. "Then what am I supposed to do? He said if I were to leave him, he would hurt me and my daughter. I stay to keep down confusion, and I know Tony will make my life miserable if I leave him."

"My father told my mother the same thing. You have to call his bluff and go get some help for you and your daughter. The house my mother lived in is empty, so if you ever want to move out of here, let me know. I had a lot of bad memories from that house, but maybe you and your daughter can turn it into a happy place to live. Just think about it, Veronica, and get away from your abuser before it's too late."

I wrote my number on a piece of paper and gave it to her. As soon as she took it, the front door opened. Both of us looked at the door, and Tony came in with a blue uniform on. It surprised me that the fool even had a job. He had a six pack of beer in his hand, while eyeing Veronica.

"How you gon' invite somebody to come inside of

this nasty motherfuckin' house? You've been sittin' on your lazy, fat ass all day, doin' nothin'. I told you about havin' company and you need to tell this bitch it's time for her to go."

Now, I wasn't Veronica, and he definitely shouldn't have gone there with me today. I was already hyped about those roses, and to be called a bitch on top of it, no, I wasn't having it.

I stood, tucking my purse underneath my arm. "Who are you calling a bitch? You don't know me, idiot, and you'd better straighten your mouth to offer me an apology."

Tony looked taken aback by my tone; after all, to him, a woman should know her place. He stepped up to me with a mean-ass mug on his face. He pointed to the door, and when Veronica spoke up about me leaving, he ordered her to shut the fuck up.

"Go get my food on the table and that shit better be hot!" Oh, hell no. It was time to put Plan B in place, and if Veronica didn't have one, I sure in the hell did. Tony turned his attention to me again. "You got ten seconds to get out of my fuckin' house, and if you don't, I'm goin' to whip yo' ass all over this livin' room like I whip hers."

My hand was already trembling by my side, and as soon as the harsh words left his mouth, I slapped the shit out of him, shaking his whole face. The slap was so loud that Veronica covered her mouth. She knew what was coming next, and so did I. He slammed his fist, into my jaw. It staggered me, and I could feel the burn. I kept my balance, though, and lifted the Mace can that I'd already had in my hand. I sprayed it in his cold eyes, and he squeezed them together. When he covered his eyes with his hand and bent down, I went at him. I used my leather Coach bag to strike his back. I kicked him in the groin, causing him to drop to his knees. The bag wasn't working enough for me, so I dropped it and started to use my fists. While trying to cool the burning in his eyes, and soreness from my kick, Tony fell flat to the floor. I took off my high heel, and used it to go upside his head. I was mad as hell. How dare this sucker think he could get away with putting his hands on me?

Veronica stood there in disbelief, and when her daughter entered the room, she yelled for her to go back to her bedroom. She in no way yelled for me to stop, though, and when I asked her to call the police, she just stood there.

"Call them, now!" I yelled, still wailing on Tony.

"Not yet," she said. She picked up a heavy, round glass ashtray, about to drop it on his head. I wasn't about to go to jail for an accessory to murder, and she was crazy if she thought I would go down with her. I quickly snatched the ashtray from her. "Your fists! Use your fists!"

Veronica used her fists to hit Tony, and as she screamed and cried while doing it, I hurried to call the police. I hated that her daughter had to witness all that was going on, but this was some shit that had to be done. The police were there within ten minutes, and when they arrived, I rushed outside. Two of them drew their guns, ordering me to get down on the ground. I did as I was told, and when another officer entered the house, he had to pull Veronica off Tony.

An officer helped me off the ground, asking what had happened. "I came to visit my friend and her boyfriend came in from work and went crazy. He jumped on me." I showed him the side of my face that

I knew had a print on it. "Luckily I had some Mace to get him off me."

The officer asked me to calm down and told me to go stand by his car. I did, and a few minutes later, they came out of the house with Tony in cuffs. He looked like a damn fool with his head hanging low and a cut on his forehead. It was dripping with blood and so was his fat lip. Seeing him in cuffs made my day, and I hoped that he'd be kept behind bars long enough for Veronica and her daughter to get the hell out of that house.

The officer put Tony in the back seat of the police car, and the other one asked me to come inside with Veronica. She and I both made Tony out to be the villain he truly was, and when they ran a police check on the fool, they found several warrants out for his arrest. He was also on probation and I suspected that he wouldn't be getting out of jail anytime soon. Thank God for that.

After the police left, Veronica, her daughter, and I sat in the living room. She apologized for getting me involved in her mess and felt bad about Tony putting his hands on me.

"I'll be fine," I said. "A little ice should take care of it. In the meantime, I'm not worried about me. I hope you stay away from him, and please, please do not let him come back here. He's going to apologize for what he did, but don't believe the hype. Even if he goes to jail, don't accept his calls. Let that fool suffer for what he's done to you."

Veronica hugged her daughter's waist and smiled. "I'm done. I assure you that I'm not going back, and it felt so good to let out my frustrations. Especially on him. I've wanted to do that for a long time, Chase, but didn't have the courage to. There's no way I'll ever put myself in a situation like that again, and I'm going to get some counseling for me and my daughter. She's only eleven years old and I'm so glad that Tony is not her biological father."

I stood up, feeling good about the deed I'd done today. Really, I wasn't a bad person, it was just that men sometimes made me crazy. Women like Claudette did too, but it was what it was.

"My offer about the house still stands. I don't know if this is his house or not, but I would be more than happy to let you see my mother's house. It's nothing spectacular, but it is much better than this place."

"If you have time tomorrow, I'd love to see it. Tony's name is on this house, and I'm looking for a fresh start for me and my daughter. I appreciate your help, and if the house doesn't work out, I can always get an apartment."

Veronica stepped forward to give me a hug. I was shocked when her daughter did as well. No one ever confirmed if her daughter had been molested by Tony, but my gut told me there was so much more to their story. I told Veronica that I'd get with her tomorrow after work, and when she asked me not to tell anyone at the job what had happened, I promised her that I wouldn't.

When I got home, I thought all of the drama for the day would be over. Unfortunately, it wasn't. Korey kept calling me, and since I ignored his calls, I knew he'd show up. In knowing so, I called Lance and asked if he would come over and take a look at my broken computer. It really wasn't broken, and when he got to my apartment and looked it over, he realized that I didn't need his assistance.

I stood in my silk pink pajama shorts and matching tank shirt. I had no bra on, so my nipples were poking through my top. I wasn't trying to entice Lance, but I needed a favor.

"There's nothing wrong with my computer, but as a friend, I need a favor," I said.

He stood in the living room, rubbing his chin with a smirk on his face. "What's up, Chase? What are you up to?"

"Korey is coming over tonight and I really don't want to be bothered. Will you stay here until he comes? Pretend that you're here with me tonight, and he'll leave once he sees that I have company."

"Are you trying to get me killed? What's up with you and that brotha?"

"Sex. Nothing more, nothing less. I can't get rid of him and he's starting to work my nerves."

"I got a feeling that you ain't trying to get rid of him. But, hey, whatever. I'm gaming. Where do you want me? In the bedroom with my clothes off or on the couch?"

I laughed and so did Lance. "Just sit on the couch. Take your shirt off, but leave your pants on."

Lance removed his shirt, and I had underestimated his frame. It wasn't all buffed and ripped or anything like that, but he did have noticeable muscles. He sat on the couch, and I placed a checkerboard on the table.

"Do you like to play checkers?" I asked.

"Sure," he said. "But first, please go put on a robe or something. I may be a friend, but first I'm a man. With your ass hanging all out of those shorts and your nipples staring at me, I don't know how much acting I can sit here and do."

I cut my eyes at Lance and went into my room to get my robe. "Is that better?" I said, covering up.

"Much better."

We started to play checkers, and almost thirty minutes later the doorbell rang. I stood up and removed the robe. I tossed it next to Lance, and he smirked while shaking his head. He rested his arms on top of the couch, waiting for me to open the door.

"Who is it?" I asked.

"You already know who it is. Open the door."

"I have company right now, Korey. I'll call you later."

"So? Screw your company. Open the door."

I paused for a moment, then opened the door. Korey looked me over. When he stepped inside, he saw Lance sitting on the couch with no expression on his face. He looked too convincing and I loved it!

"Do you want me to leave?" Lance asked.

"No, baby. Stay right there."

Korey stood in awe. His hands were in his pockets and he cut his eyes at me. "Why haven't you been answering your phone? I've been calling you all day."

I glanced over at Lance, then back at Korey. "Can't you see? I've been busy. What is it that you want?"

"I just wanted to tell you that I did not send those flowers to Claudette. I was only playing with you earlier, and when I spoke to my mother, she told me she sent them. Now what?"

"Nothing. You assumed that I was jealous, but I wasn't. I really don't give a damn who sent them, but as I said, I'm busy tonight. You need to stop showing up like this, and it is such an inconvenience for me to have to explain our relationship to Lance."

"I know that's right," Lance added. "And I ain't happy about what's going on, either."

"Then step," Korey suggested. "I need to talk to her about some things anyway, and I'm sure you already got what you came here for."

"I always do," Lance spat. "And since I'm right across the hall, I can have access anytime I want to. As for tonight, I'm not leaving, you are. Quickly state your business, chump, as I'm in a hurry to conduct mine."

I wanted to crack up from the look on Korey's face. Men were something else, especially the ones who were in relationships with other people. I knew he didn't think he had it like that with me, did he? As he stood there looking stupid, I guessed he was starting to get the picture that good dick could in no way win me over. What one man could do, there was always another one who could do it better.

"Cool," Korey said to Lance. "Have your fun tonight, but since you and Chase got this open relationship going on, I hope she told you about our time at the Christmas party that night. If you've been so good to her, then why was she off in another room fucking me? You ain't all that, brotha, and don't think that this is the last you'll see of me."

"I suspect not, and, as a matter of fact, she did tell me about that night. Said it wasn't as satisfying as she had hoped it would be. I had to pick up where you left off."

"Wait a minute," I said. Now they were starting to go too far. Korey had no business telling what we'd done at the Christmas party. How dare he try to bust me out, especially when I hadn't said one word to Claudette? And Lance shouldn't have said that Korey wasn't satisfying. I knew I'd want some of that dick at a later date, so I had to quickly clear things up. "I need both of you to exit tonight. I got a headache right now, and I am in no mood to deal with this."

Lance got up from the couch, tossing his shirt over his shoulder. He stepped to the door and placed his finger underneath my chin to lift it. "I'll see you tomorrow, cupcake. Sleep well." He placed a juicy kiss on my lips, and adding a little something extra, he patted my ass. I was in no way mad, but he didn't have to go so far. Korey watched Lance exit, and when he closed the door, Korey still didn't want to leave.

"What do you want me to do?" he asked. "I apologize for joking with you earlier. I can't believe you can't take a joke."

I opened the door. "Well, this isn't a joke, Korey. I'm tired and I want you to leave. Don't make me sit here and argue with you about this. I truly felt as if our relationship would never reach this level. You're starting to turn me off and disappointment me. Don't."

He pouted and left like a whiny child who couldn't have his way. Maybe he and Claudette had more in common than I'd thought. The childish behavior was, indeed, working me.

Chapter 5

The week went by pretty quickly. Friday was here before I knew it, and by then, Veronica was back to work. She seemed much better, and after I had shown her my mother's house the other day, she couldn't wait to move in. I hadn't been to the house in months, because every time I went there it brought back bad memories of my father inappropriately touching me. Paid for or not, I would never live there again. Still, it was good to know that the house wouldn't just sit there and go to waste.

At first, I didn't even want to go inside, but when I saw how excited Veronica's daughter was about the size of her new room, I felt at ease. The walls needed to be painted, and I had some plumbing work that needed to be done. Other than that, Veronica agreed to pay me $900 a month for rent, and she and I signed a rental agreement yesterday. I told her I'd help her paint the rooms, so we made arrangements to take care of that on Saturday. I asked if she'd heard from Tony, and she said he hadn't called at all. She was so anxious to move from that house, but I made her promise to take care of mine. Even though I had some bad memories there, I still didn't want a tenant who intended to mess it up.

I left for lunch, and went to the bank to cash my check. I kept reminding myself to call a certain financial planner so he could help me budget my money better, and when I pulled my car over, I searched for Steven's business card in my purse. I dialed his number, but his secretary answered the phone.

"I would like to make an appointment to speak with Mr. Smith about financial planning."

"Are you a new client?"

"Yes, I am. He was highly recommended by a friend."

"Okay," she said. "Let me check his calendar." She paused for a moment, then spoke up. "How does next Friday sound? I can pencil you in for eleven o'clock."

"You don't have anything sooner? I was hoping to get in sooner."

"Normally, he doesn't come in on the weekends, but if that's the only time you can make it, I'll see if he can do a Saturday or Sunday afternoon."

"Sunday would be great. Maybe around four or five?"

She put me on hold, and when she came back to the phone, she confirmed four o'clock on Sunday. She gave me directions to his office, and also gave me a list of things to bring. I thanked her and ended the call.

Before heading back to work, I stopped by the Galleria to get a pair of shoes I'd seen early on in the week. Just as I was leaving, I spotted Drake's black Lincoln MKS parked in the parking lot, near The Cheesecake Factory. Since he hadn't called me, I guess he had sobered up and was mad at me for setting his house on fire. I had gotten over it, but when I looked inside of the restaurant and saw him sitting at a table with a woman, it infuriated me.

I didn't know if she was a client of his, but by the way he was smiling and touching her hand, I suspected not. I didn't want him to see me, so I quickly walked away from the window. I looked through my keys, searching for one that had the sharpest point on the end. When I found it, I slowly walked beside his car, pressing hard on the key and causing it to scrape off the paint. The key left long, deep scratches, and it looked pretty good against his black shiny car. I smiled, and hurried back to work so I wouldn't be late. When I got there, the receptionist stopped me in the lobby.

"Chase, these came for you while you were at lunch."

I looked at the bouquet of red roses, and smiled because I knew who they were from. I read the card;

Answer your phone and talk to me, please. Can't stop thinking about you, and if we have to play by your rules, so be it.

Sounded like a plan to me, and I couldn't wait until the day was over so I could thank Korey like I wanted to. The moment I got back to my desk, Claudette was already on her feet, and so was Veronica.

"Somebody's in love," Claudette said. "Are those from Lance?"

"No," I said. "They're from someone else. Someone special and someone I truly admire."

Veronica poked me in my side. "You need to stop keeping secrets from us. I'm going to find out who this mystery man of yours is, and you won't be able to keep him a secret for long."

"No, she won't. Not as nosy as we are, and you

should be proud to speak about a man who gives you flowers. Korey is . . ."

I knew Claudette would throw Korey into this, and as she went on and on, I sniffed the roses and excused myself to go call him. I went to the closed-in stairway that was an emergency exit. I sat on the concrete stairs and dialed his cell phone number.

"It's about damn time," he said. "Are you happy now? I purchased those myself, and I assure you that my mother had nothing to do with it."

"Flowers don't move me, Korey, but the thought was nice. I'm just horny and I figured you would be too. See you around eight and don't be late."

"Not a chance."

"Not a minute earlier, either. I have some stops to make, so don't expect me to be there until eight."

Korey hung up on me, but that was fine with me. I expected him to arrive at eight, and I wasn't surprised when the knock on my door came at 7:59 P.M. I was already naked, and when I opened the door, I took Korey's hand and pulled him inside. I closed the door and cornered him in front of the door. My eyes searching his said exactly what I wanted, and I wasted no time removing his jacket and belt. I unzipped his jeans and, as I lowered them to his ankles, I kneeled in front of him. I had never given him oral sex before, but I felt up to it tonight. My mouth went into action, and I soaked him with my saliva. I tightened my jaws, giving extra attention to his head that was so sensitive. My hand was working with the rhythm of my mouth, and as I sped up my movement, Korey's legs were weakening. I massaged his sacks while listening to him moan loudly.

"I am so fucked up," he admitted. "What are you doing to me? Suck this dick, baby. Thank you for sucking this muthafucka like this. Damn, you're good. Too, too good."

He pumped himself into my mouth, and as I felt his dick pulsating, I backed my mouth away from it. I used the swift strokes of my hand to bring him to an eruption, and it was a good one, too. His lava oozed out, dripping down my hand like a hot volcano.

"Damn," was all he could say. He gripped his dick to calm it, and I watched his ripped stomach heave in and out. I stood up, and picked up a towel from the table to wipe my hands.

That night, I was spent and so was Korey. We had done the wild thing all over my apartment, and were now in my bedroom, sprawled out on my bed. I was tired as ever, more so because I couldn't get any sleep. Korey's phone was ringing off the hook all night, and he had finally gotten up around three o'clock in the morning to turn it off. That allowed me to get a little sleep, but by morning, I was still feeling sluggish. I definitely didn't feel like painting today, but I told Veronica I would help her, so I had to get up.

"Why are you up so early?" Korey asked.

"It's already nine o'clock, and I told a friend of mine that I'd help her paint."

Korey yawned and moved to the edge of the bed. As I walked by him, he grabbed my waist and sat me on his lap. "Have you thought about what I said?" he asked.

"You've said a lot. What specifically are you referring to?"

"About us hooking up as a couple. I'm feeling this,

Chase, and I want to start doing some things with you, outside of this apartment. Personally, I think we can have a good relationship and I'm ready to do this."

"What about Claudette? She would never accept you leaving her, especially for me. You would make work hectic for me, and I don't want to go to work fighting with her about us being together."

"Then, what do you want me to do? I refuse to be with a woman who I'm not feeling much for anymore, and you, yourself, recommended that I tell her how I feel."

"I don't care if you tell her how you feel or not, but just don't tell her about me. It would really cause problems for me, and I don't know if I can handle that right now. Give this a little more time, okay?"

"I think you want more time because you don't want to give up old boy across the hall. Are you in love with him?"

I stood up and pecked Korey's lips. "If I were in love with anyone, I wouldn't be in this bed with you. My relationship with him isn't that serious, and he's only there for convenience. When I'm alone, I call him."

"But you don't have to be alone. You can be with me, and, trust me, this shit will work. You have yet to acknowledge our connection. Why are we letting what we feel for each other go to waste?"

"We won't. But, just don't rush this. I want to be sure that this is the right thing to do. When I'm able to look Claudette in the eyes and tell her that I've fallen in love with you, then we'll make some changes. Right now, I'm not in love. I do, however, feel our connection, but it's not enough for me right now. In time, maybe so."

Korey and I cleaned up in the shower, and, like always, being with him in that manner was nice. Still, I

was in no way ready for what he wanted. If he continued to turn up the pressure, I'd have to put Plan B in
place, and that consisted of getting rid of him.

Veronica decided to keep it simple. She wanted all
white walls, so we painted them room by room. Now,
give or take, there were only seven rooms in the house,
but the bedrooms weren't that small. The kitchen wasn't
either, so it took us longer than expected. By four
o'clock, I realized that I should have gotten someone
to help us, so doing what I knew best, I called Lance.
He was already out and about. He said that he could
be there within the hour. I couldn't believe how nice
he'd been to me, and I appreciated his friendship so
much. I realized that we had a lot in common. Just the
other day, he'd stepped into the hallway with his cell
phone, asking me to answer it.

Apparently, he didn't want to talk to the woman on
the other end, and he was trying to get rid of her. I told
the woman that I was at his apartment, and I was his
woman. She called me all kinds of names and hung up
on me. Lance said that he'd been trying to ditch her
for months, but she didn't know how to take no for an
answer. We laughed about the games we were playing,
and I told him if he ever needed me again to let me
know. The same went for him.

Veronica knew that Lance and I were just neighbors, so I asked if she wanted me to hook her up. I
made it clear to her that he was a dog, but Veronica
said she was just looking for someone to have some
fun with. When Lance arrived, she was all smiles. She
insisted that he was so handsome to her, and as he
started to paint the hallway with his shirt off, she
pulled me aside.

"Please tell him that I want to hook up with him," she whispered.

"Calm down," I said. "I promise to get around to it."

I had seen Lance's taste in women, and it was just okay. Veronica was a very pretty girl, but I wasn't sure about her size.

"Whew," I said, sitting on the floor, wiping the sweat from my forehead. Veronica sat next to me, sweating profusely as well. It was a good thing that her daughter wasn't there with us; if she had been, she would have passed out from heat exhaustion.

Lance stepped down from the ladder and stood in front of us. "Why y'all sitting down being lazy? We are almost finished, and after I finish, there are one and a half rooms left to go."

I fell back on the floor, sighing from the thought of painting one more room. I wanted my bed so badly, and I couldn't wait to get home. "Can't you finish the rest?" I asked Lance. "We've been at this all day and my arms feel as if they are about to fall off."

"Mine too," Veronica said. "Maybe we can come back tomorrow."

That would cut into my time with Steven, so hell no, we weren't coming back tomorrow. We were finishing up today.

Lance picked up a bucket of paint. "I don't mind finishing up, but I'm about to run out of paint. If somebody will go with me to get another bucket, I'll have this done in no time."

I was gaming for that, and I opted to go with Lance. We hadn't eaten anything all day, so I got Veronica's order for Chinese food. As Lance and I drove to Home Depot, I turned down the music so I could tell him Veronica was interested.

"Hey, Lance. What do you think of my friend Veronica?"

"She seems nice. This is only the second time I've seen her, but I can tell she's a sweet person."

"Is she cute?"

"Very."

"Would you be interested in taking her on a date?"

He shrugged his shoulders, but didn't comment yet.

"She said that she likes you. Could you see yourself being with someone like her?"

He shrugged again. "I'm not really sure, but personally, I kind of like somebody else."

"You like a whole lot of people," I laughed, referring to the women I'd seen at his house. "But I'm just curious if you'd take her on a date."

"Nah, I don't think that would be a good idea."

"Why not? I think the two of you would have fun."

He parked his truck in the Home Depot parking lot and turned off the engine. "It's wouldn't be a good idea because I'm digging a close friend of hers. There's no doubt that I'd have fun with Veronica, but I think I'd have so much more fun with you."

For whatever reason, I was stunned. Lance and I seemed to have this cute little brother-sister thing going on, and I didn't think he was interested in me in such a way. I pointed to myself. "Me. You're interested in dating me?"

"Yep. Why not you?"

"Because . . ." I really couldn't think of a reason, but I said, "No. You shouldn't want to date a woman like me. You and I both play too many games. It would be a mess. I can't believe you suggested something so ridiculous."

"Okay," Lance said, getting out of the car. "Just hurt

my damn feelings. I guess it was a ridiculous thought, but, at the time, it seemed like a good one."

I locked Lance's arm with mine and laughed as we walked toward Home Depot. "I wasn't trying to hurt your feelings, but we're so . . . so, you know, cool. Don't you think we're cool?"

"Cool as a fan. Now, back away so I can pick up my face from the ground, since you cracked it."

I laughed, keeping my arm locked with his. "Lance," I whined.

"What?" he whined back.

"I'm sorry. I'll think about it, okay?"

"Fine. Now, let's go get this paint so I can finish up. I got a date tonight, and wait until you see this one. She makes Halle Berry look like a seven."

I shoved his shoulder. "Well, I make her look like a six. In that case, your date couldn't be all that."

Lance laughed, but agreed.

We didn't finish up until ten o'clock that night. I told Veronica that Lance was really digging someone else and he wanted to give his relationship with her a fair chance. Yes, I lied, but I didn't want to hurt Veronica's feelings. Even so, when we got home, I peeped through my peephole to check out Lance's date. She had nothing on Halle Berry, but she definitely wasn't short stopping. I watched her go inside his apartment, and about twenty minutes after that, they left. Lance's personality alone made him attractive. As I'd said, he wasn't turning a lot of heads, but when women got to know him, I understood how they could easily fall for him. I thought about what he'd said, and I intended to keep it in mind. For now, though, I had a full plate with Korey, and any room left on that plate would be for Steven.

* * *

I was well rested and excited about my appointment today. I gathered all of the papers Steven's secretary had asked me to bring, and made sure everything was in order. That included my attire. I wore a powder blue silk pencil skirt and blue blouse that draped in the front, showing my meaty cleavage. My tall black heels gave me much height, and my ponytail was wrapped in a bun. I left the bangs on my forehead, and put my silver dangling earrings in my ears. I sprayed on a few dashes of sweet perfume, and added a bit more mascara to my lashes that were already thick and pretty. My hazel eyes were so addictive, and as I stared in the mirror, I hoped that my good looks would work in my favor.

When I arrived at Steven's office, there was no receptionist out front. A bell was on the counter, so I hit the bell to let someone know I was there. A few minutes later, Steven swooped around a corner with a cell phone on his ear.

"Please have a seat," he said. "I'll be with you shortly."

Just that fast, a drip of juice trickled in my panties. Well, not quite in my panties, because I wasn't wearing any. Let's just say I felt myself getting moist, and the way Steven was looking, I was sure the wetness would increase. He really had that swagga like Denzel, if not, better. The deep blue suit he wore had a silky shine to it, and his flowing black waves were lined to perfection. The gray in his beard made him look so masculine and sexy. Liz really did have herself some serious eye candy. Waking up to him every morning had to be a good feeling, and I couldn't wait for my turn to wake up with him by my side.

As I sat in thought, Steven came out of the room and stood in front of me. He extended his hand, revealing his pearly whites. "I hope the wait wasn't too long. Chase Jenkins, right?"

"Yes." I smiled with glee. "Chase Jenkins."

"Follow me," he said. He put his hands in his pockets, and as he walked in front of me, I couldn't help but notice his nice ass. I had a vision of it in motion.

Steven invited me to take a seat in the chair in front of his mahogany desk, then offered to get me something to drink.

"Soda, water, wine," he joked. "Not wine, just kidding. But if you'd like something to drink, I'll get it for you."

No, he wasn't kidding, and neither was I. "Actually, wine sounds good, but I'll save the celebration for another day. For now, bottled water would be fine."

Steven winked and left his office. Maybe this wasn't going to be as hard as I thought, as his eyes were flirting with me already. Before he came back into his office, I pulled the dip in the front of my blouse a little lower, and inched up my skirt before I took a seat. I crossed my moisturized legs, showing some of the thickness of my thighs. Steven came back into the room, setting a glass of ice and bottled water in front of me.

"Thank you," I said, watching him take his seat.

"You're welcome. Now, how can I help you today?"

There were a slew of answers to that question, but, for now, I went with the more appropriate answer. "Mr. Smith, I really don't make an enormous amount of money, but what little I do make, I need to figure out how to budget better. Basically, I need my money to start working for me. I don't have any children, and I do have some money set aside in a bank account that my deceased mother left me. I'm cautious about how I spend that money, and I wondered if you could help me with planning how to invest it correctly, as well as save all that I can for my retirement."

"I'd love to help. I talk to young people all the time about how they can make their money work for them. Believe it or not, it doesn't require a lot of money to do it. You just have to be smart about where your money goes. You'd be surprised how much excess money you let fly out the window. I'm going to show you how you can use that money to invest, and like you said, save for your retirement. I see you have an envelope in your hand. Did you bring everything my secretary asked you to bring?"

"Yes, I did." I passed the papers over to him. Before he looked into the envelope, he laid it in front of him.

"Before I look at your information, I want to discuss ways that I can help you and share with you how my partners and I operate. All of us are risk takers, and we basically built this company from the ground by taking risk. I will recommend that when it comes to investing your money, you do the same. I know you're my wife's assistant, but your information, as well as anything that we discuss, will always remain confidential."

That was good to know, and as Steven started to tell me about his business, I listened . . . for a moment, at least, and then I started thinking about where I wanted to fuck him. He seemed like a hotel kind of man, but then again, his office would suit us just fine. It had a couch, a huge desk, and the round table wasn't a bad idea either. I could never take him to my apartment, and I doubted that he'd invite me to his house.

Then again, as good as I'd be to him, anything was possible.

As he went on, I sipped my water. I batted my eyes at him and kept good posture so my perky breasts couldn't be ignored. After a while, I got bored with his talking and I interrupted him.

"I'm sorry, Mr. Smith, but I have to use the restroom. Is there one nearby?"

"Yes. It's right outside my door to your left. You can't miss it, and take your time. I need to return a quick call to Liz, and it shouldn't be long."

I stood, straightening my pencil skirt and turning so he could get a glimpse of my curvaceous backside. I sauntered away to the restroom, checking myself in the mirror again to make sure everything was in order. I glossed my lips with more M•A•C, and tugged at the front of my blouse again. Damn, I was gorgeous and there was no denying it.

I washed my hands, then headed back to Steven's office. He was still on the phone, and before I took a seat, I moved the chair back just a little. I sat with my legs slightly opened, and when I noticed his eyes drop between my legs, I hurried to cross them.

"Okay, Liz," he said. "That sounds fine. See you later."

He hung up and rubbed his hands together. "Sorry about that. Now, where were we?"

"You were telling me about all that you could do for me. I've been listening, Mr. Smith, but I have to be honest with you about some things. I really don't think you are the financial planner I'm looking for." I opened my legs again, then slowly switched my leg to the other side. Yeah, I was doing the Sharon Stone thing like in the movie *Basic Instinct*, and Steven's eyes were zoned in.

He blinked, then looked at my eyes. They were just as addictive. "Why . . . why don't you think I can help you? I assured you that any business we conduct, it will remain confidential."

"I notice that you keep stressing that, and I hope that our business does remain confidential. Not the kind of business that you may have in mind, but let me go ahead and be as up front with you as I possibly can. I didn't come here for you to be my financial planner. I liked what I saw at the Christmas party, and I made a mental note to reach out to you. Today, I'm reaching out, simply because my panties get wet every time I see you. I hoped you wouldn't let all of this excitement I'm feeling for you go to waste, and I'd be grateful if you'd be willing to help me resolve my issues."

Steven massaged his chin and slowly stood up. "Listen, young lady, I don't have time for games. I'm sure that my wife sent you here. It is so tacky of you to come in here, presenting yourself to me this way. I'll take care of Liz when I get home, but you need to leave my office, immediately."

I remained in my seat. "I assure you that Liz knows nothing about this. I don't play games either, and I am as serious as a heart attack about this. If you would like me to show you just how serious I am, I'm willing to do that too. And if you still believe that your wife would be foolish enough to send a woman like me to your office with no panties on, and allow her to fuck your brains out, then you're a fool."

He in no way seemed convinced, so I stood up and unzipped my skirt from behind. I eased it past my curvy hips, letting it drop to the floor. My blouse was in no way long enough to cover my goods, so my bottom half was completely exposed. Steven stood in awe. His eyes followed me as I walked around his desk and sat on top of it. I scooted over so he could stand right between my legs and he did not move. Having his attention, I cocked my legs a little wider, allowing him to at least see my clit.

"There," I said. "Is this better? Do you think, for one second, Liz would recommend that I come here and do this? I don't think so, Mr. Smith, and if you want to lower your pants, I'm sure one of us can find a condom."

He swallowed the lump in his throat and inched backward. I wasn't sure if it was to get a better glimpse of my pussy, but he sure as hell looked. He still was hesitant, so just to get him going, I reached down and touched the soft, trimmed hair on my pussy. I dipped my finger into me and could see Steven's breathing increase.

"Do you believe me now?" I moaned. "You've got me wet like this, Steven; don't you want to fuck me? I want you so badly and—"

"Stop it!" he yelled, then turned around to face the windows that were covered with blinds. "Leave. Please, leave."

I figured he wouldn't go for it the first time around, but I hadn't expected to get this far with him. I did, however, intend to leave something on his mind, and as I removed myself from his desk, he turned to take a glance at my backside. I bent over to pick up my skirt, and noticed him close his eyes. I eased into my skirt, and when I picked up my purse, I headed for the door.

"Chase," he said, halting my steps.

"Yes." I turned with a smirk on my face.

"Don't ever come back here again. Got it?"

"If you say so."

"And don't call me at this number again. I have your number, and I'll call you. Soon."

I smiled, and wanted to blow that fine muthafucka a kiss. "I hope so," was all I could say.

Chapter 6

A beautiful woman such as myself could have any-thing in life she wanted. A decent job, money, a nice car, friends if she wanted them, and definitely the man of her choice. Thing was, she couldn't have a faithful man, and all of the men I have known, and met over the years, had proven that statement to be true. Faithful men didn't exist in my book, and as long as I was smart enough to realize that, my life as I lived it was just fine. I knew what to expect from men, and there was no need for me to shed tears if my relation-ships didn't work out.

In no way was I willing to give 100 percent of myself to anyone. No man was deserving, and when Steven had called me the other night, I put a check by his name on my to-do list. He was already a done deal, but I had to play my cards even better with him. I knew I could get too attached to a man like him, so I was careful. He wanted to meet me at a hotel that night, and as soon as he called and told me he was there, I canceled. Told him that something came up, and I'd have to shoot for another day. He accused me of playing around with him, but in a sense, I wasn't. I just wanted to make sure I called the shots, not him. I told him that I wanted to meet at his office, specifically because he told me not to come back there. He wasn't too thrilled about it, but said he'd call me Friday night after work.

With that, I was giddy as ever at work on Friday. We had a nine o'clock meeting, and anything Liz asked me to do, I happily abided. When the meeting was over, Veronica and I sat around talking about how excited she and her daughter were to be in my house. I was delighted that she'd made such an imperative move.

As for Claudette, well, she wasn't looking too good these days. I had backed off Korey just a little bit, but we still saw each other. He wasn't pressuring me as much, either, but as far as I knew, the wedding was still on. Claudette wasn't talking about it as much, but she was still talking about it enough. I invited her to go to lunch with me and Veronica, just to find out what, if anything, was going on in her personal life that involved me. We sat at Applebees waiting for our lunch to be served.

"Claudette, your wedding is just around the corner. You don't seem as excited as you were before, but have you decided where you and Korey are going for your honeymoon?" I asked.

"We have plans to go to Jamaica." She shrugged. "But Korey always changes his mind about things at the last minute."

"Jamaica sounds like fun," I said. "And if I were getting married, that's where I would go too." She gave me a fake grin. I touched her hand, appearing to be concerned. "Are you okay? I'm used to you being so spirited and upbeat. What's wrong?"

She sighed, and I could tell Veronica and I were about to get an earful. "I'm okay. It's just that Korey's been acting kind of strange lately. When I ask him if everything is okay, he says that it is. I know my man, and I can tell that he's not being completely honest with me. I really want to know how a woman can tell if her man is cheating."

I was blunt. "If you have to ask, then, yes, he's cheating. I don't know much about Korey, but you know him better than I do."

Veronica added her two cents. "I don't trust men, period. And Korey is rather good-looking. I hope you've been keeping your eyes on him."

"I have, especially lately. When I call him, he never answers his phone. We barely have sex anymore, and when we do, I'm the one who has to initiate it. I don't mean to be putting all of my business out there like this, but he tried some freaky mess on me and I'm not in to all of that stuff."

"Freaky stuff like what?" I inquired. I definitely knew what she was talking about, as Korey had a wild side to him that surprised even me. A woman like Claudette didn't know how to step up to the plate, and Korey was falling for me because I had mad skills.

"I'm too embarrassed to say it. I recently started having oral sex with him, and that in itself was a bit much for me."

"What?" Veronica and I both said in unison. "What's so wrong with oral sex?" I asked.

Claudette's face scrunched up. "It's nasty. I don't want to put his private parts in my mouth, and the thought of some of that stuff seeping into my mouth is gross. I do like when he goes down on me, but just knowing what comes out of me, on a monthly basis, it doesn't seem right for him to be down there, either."

Veronica was shaking her head, and I definitely knew why. Maybe if she would wash up down below, she wouldn't trip off something so stupid. "Claudette," I said. "If you don't give that man what he wants, someone else will. Oral sex is a big . . . huge part of making love to your man, and every man I've ever met wants head. It's not an option anymore, and if you plan to be his wife, you'd better get over it. Not to hurt your feelings, but he very well may be seeing someone else, especially since you're not giving him what he wants."

"I do," she said, defending herself. "Just not that or any of that freaky stuff he likes to do. Other than that, we're good. I pray that he's not slipping away from me. I don't know what I'm going to do if I find out he's seeing someone else."

"Kill her and him," Veronica laughed. "He's engaged to you, and nothing like that should really be going on. Maybe you're just blowing things out of proportion, especially since it's getting so close to your wedding day. Are you possibly getting cold feet?"

"No," Claudette said, watching the waiter put her food in front of her. He served Veronica and me as well, then refilled our drinks.

"Will there be anything else, ladies?"

"No," we all said.

"Enjoy," the waiter replied, and walked away from the table.

I was hungry, so I quickly dove into my food. So did Veronica, but Claudette was picking at her salad. "I just love him so much," she said. "I hope my gut is lying to me, but you know what they say: your gut never lies."

"I can vouch for that," I said, thinking about Drake. "When I had that feeling, it was definitely the truth. Just keep your eyes on him, and if anything seems out of the ordinary, call him on it. As a matter of fact, you should tell him how you feel and see how he responds. You'll be able to pick up on any vibes, and pretty much go from there."

Claudette nodded and we continued to talk while eating our food.

I sat at my desk, rubbing my full belly. I had really overdone it at the restaurant, and had the nerve to order cheesecake. The slice was huge, and even though I'd shared, the bulk of it was in my belly.

Ever since we'd gotten back from lunch, Liz had been in her office. Her phone calls were on hold, because earlier she'd said that she had to get something done for Mr. Aimes, who owned the refrigeration company we worked for. I asked if I could help, but Liz felt as if she'd already given me enough to do. I couldn't agree with her more, and as I started to type some of the letters she'd given me to type, the phone rang. I answered, and hearing his voice made me squirm in my seat.

"Is Liz there?" Steven asked.

"She is, but she's in her office with the door closed. Her calls are transferred to me because she's working on a project for Mr. Aimes."

"That's fine. I just wanted to tell her that I am working late tonight. I guess you know why. I hope you're not going to stand me up again."

"No, I'm not. Eight o'clock, right?"

"Yep. See you soon."

I hung up and got back to finishing my papers for Liz.

As always, when five o'clock came around, I rushed out of the office. I withdrew some money from the ATM, stopped at the mall to get another pair of shoes I wanted, then went home to get ready for my night. It was a Friday night, so I expected that Korey would want to come over. Instead of him calling to bug me, I called him. I told him that I was going to my cousin's baby shower, and I couldn't believe that he didn't question me. He told me to enjoy myself, and said that he'd call me tomorrow.

By seven-thirty, I was on my way to Steven's office. This time, I wore a one-piece stretch dress that was easy for him to pull in any direction he wished. My hair was in a bun like the last time I'd seen him, and the only reason I wore it that way was because it made me look more conservative. No, I was in no way conservative, but the look worked for Steven. I couldn't wait to see what he was working with, so I sped up to get to his office. When I got there, the inside was near dark. I opened the glass front door to the lobby, and just to be on the safe side, I locked it behind me. I made my way around the corner to Steven's office, and his door was already opened. He sat behind his desk, dressed to impress with a brown pinstriped suit on. The only light in the room was the one on his desk. I could see his handsome face, but it was serious as ever. At first, I thought he'd changed his mind, until I got closer and saw his grin come into play.

"I don't like us meeting here," he said. "My partners

can come in here anytime. Let me take you to a hotel. We'll have much more room than we will in here."

I removed my coat and laid it on the chair. "I locked the front door, and I'm one who likes to work with whatever space I have. Get used to it, especially if we intend to make this an ongoing thing."

Steven stood and removed his jacket. He wiggled his multicolored silk tie away from his neck and took off his shirt. "It depends on you if there will be a next time. Not me."

I watched as Steven got undressed and I did the same thing. Now, I know I'd been bragging about how well Korey was packing, but the size of Steven's thing really put Korey to shame. That thing was huge, and it looked plump as ever. He did, however, have this unsure look on his face, and I knew it was my job to put him at ease.

He took a seat on the tan plush leather sofa and dropped a condom on the table beside it. I picked up the condom, but before I put it on him, I straddled his lap on my knees. His hard dick was resting between my legs, but I didn't let it enter me. I placed my arms on his shoulders and looked into his deep, yet serious, pretty eyes.

"Relax," I suggested. "I know you're not comfortable with this, but it's okay for you to have *some* fun, isn't it? Trust me, you will."

I scooted back a bit, placing the condom over Steven's hardness. I returned to my position on his lap, swaying back and forward to lace his dick with my trickling wetness. I still hadn't let him enter me, but was teasing him with the feel of my slit. His hands roamed around my curves, and when he massaged my ass, my insides started to burn. My breasts were right at his lips, and as he circled his tongue around my nipples, my coochie was starting to drip more. He pulled my ass cheeks apart, slightly lifting me to the tip of his dick. I jolted down on it, and an instant arch formed in my back.

"Ohh, shit," I warned as if Steven had split me wide open. I felt every inch of him, and for the moment, I couldn't even move.

"Uh-huh," he gloated. "I know you didn't expect not to feel that, did you?"

"I did," I whispered. "But not like that."

Steven continued to hold my cheeks apart, slowly guided me up and down on his shaft. That thing was deep in my gut, but was feeling amazingly good. The gushier my insides got, the easier it became for me to slide on him. I started to get my rhythm, and formed a deeper arch in my back. Instead of holding my butt cheeks, he held my waist so I could stay on top of him. I jolted up and down on him, and my breasts were bouncing like balls. They were tight as ever, and when Steven sucked them, they felt even tighter. We were starting to connect, and as he pumped into me, I pumped back, giving him everything I had.

"Umph, umph, umph," he groaned while massaging my curvy backside again. "Wha... what a damn shame. You make me feel as if I've been missing out on something."

"That's because you have," I confirmed. "But if I can help it, not anymore."

For the first time tonight, I leaned in to kiss Steven. His lips were soft as butter, and the way he lightly turned his tongue in my mouth was stimulating.

"Mmmmm," he said, holding the sides of my face while kissing me. He took a few bites on my lips and when he slowed his pumping inside of me, I slowly stood up. His dick plopped out of me, long, dripping wet, and still very hard. I faced the front of the couch, and then bent over so I could feel him from behind. He found his spot, and I had never had a man work me so well in this position. I kneeled forward on the couch, and hiked my ass up as far as it would go. My knees were separated, and Steven was forcing my insides further and further apart with each thrust.

"Fuck," I shouted, wanting to pull my hair from my head. "I'm hurting, but please don't stop. Harder, Steven, fuck me harder."

Steven was slamming into me with everything he had. And from one position to the next, we fucked each other as if we both had something to prove. His phone was ringing, but he in no way had time to answer it. It was a battle to the finish line, and after going at it for so long, I threw in the towel, coming for the third time that night. I cut up so bad that Steven had to cover my mouth with his to silence me. I asked if he'd come too, and he lowered my hand so I could feel the overly filled condom.

"I didn't have to let it be known like you, but you did your thing. I'm pleased that you reached out to me, and I look forward to you reaching out to me again."

He pecked my lips, then lifted his body off mine. "I need to get home. I'm sure when the phone was ringing, it was Liz calling to see why I hadn't made it home yet." He walked over to his desk, and picked up the clock, holding it in his hand.

"Funny how time flies when you're having so much fun. Can you believe it's almost eleven o'clock already?"

I was already putting on my clothes. I knew it was

time to wrap things up, but this was one time that I could have gone a few more rounds. I had to come prepared for Steven, and since he said it was left up to me about seeing him again, I planned on reaching out to him . . . tomorrow.

The next day, I was too hung over from the sex Steven had put on me. I didn't bother to call him, and I was surprised that I hadn't heard from Korey, either. Something was definitely up with him, but at this point, I really didn't care. I had Steven on my mind, and as far as I was concerned, it was time to wrap up my rendezvous with Korey as quickly as I could. I enjoyed being by myself on the weekend, that was, until I saw Lance coming up the steps.

I had just taken out the trash and he invited me to his apartment so we could play cards. A bit bored, I joined him. He and I had a good time eating peanuts and playing spades. After a while, we started playing UNO. I beat him at almost every hand, but he insisted that he'd let me win. The whole time I was at his apartment, his phone stayed busy. Not once did Lance answer, but when I asked why he wasn't answering his phone, he said that he needed a break from the hassles with women.

"Sometimes, this playing thing gets old, but the women in my life can't deny that I've always been honest with them about each other."

"I don't know if that really helps, but no one can knock you for being honest. I try to be honest too, because it's no fun being lied to."

Lance chuckled, and since he forgot to say "UNO," I made him pick up two cards. "Damn," he laughed. "I got sidetracked. But, uh, how many men are you see-

ing right now? I know you still creeping with ol' boy,
but I haven't seen anyone else around lately."

I smiled, thinking about Steven. "I'm doing some
things away from home, and I suspect that Korey's
face will soon be limited. It's definitely time to move
on to bigger and better things."

"Happens to me all the time," Lance said, giving me
a high five.

The weekend was over, and already it was back to
work for me. I wasn't sure how I'd feel about seeing
Liz. Had I known she was the one with the man who
could make me see fireworks, I would have opted for
him first. I figured he would be as experienced as he
was, and most of the time, older men were. They sure
knew how to bring their A game. I wasn't trying to
knock Korey at all. He was definitely on the right path,
and in ten more years, I was sure he'd be able to have
those moves like Steven. It was kind of strange, too,
because Steven hadn't even gone down on me. I couldn't
wait for that to happen, and I would, without a doubt,
return the favor.

I was so hyped about my weekend that when I got to
work, I didn't even realize it was Valentine's Day. The
women were all running around, trying to see who
was going to get what. This had to be the most stupid
holiday of the year. The last time I checked, there was
no need to set aside one day of the year to express your
love for someone. The flowers and cards should be
flowing throughout the year, and it was so sad for
some women to depend on getting something for that
one single day out of the year. I guess some people had
something to prove, and the first person to open her
big mouth was Claudette. Since I had slacked up on

seeing Korey, I noticed another attitude change in her. She was perky again, and no one had to ask me why.

"Korey gave me a big ol' box of candies last night and took me to dinner. It was so nice, and you know we had a wonderful time last night. I bought that Chrisette Michele CD, and we listened to that thing all night long."

I knew what she was getting at, but Veronica said it. "You mean y'all made love all night long. Get it right, Claudette, and stop beating around the bush."

She smiled and patted herself on the back. "I'm back in action," she bragged. "Korey is too."

I thought it was so ridiculous for her to sit around at work, discussing her sex life, especially with a man she planned to marry. No doubt, if you advertise your man's goods as much as Claudette did, then some women will want to taste those goods. Me being one of them. Claudette had been setting herself up for the longest time, and whatever she had coming to her, she deserved it. Of course, it irritated me that she and Korey were back into action, but just a tiny bit. I did like Korey, but I figured he was upset with me because I wasn't going to give him what he wanted. If I did, I could snatch him from Claudette in a heartbeat. After what she'd said, I wasn't 100 percent sure that I was done with him yet. I so wanted to see her get her face cracked, but timing was everything. In due time that would definitely happen.

As we stood by Claudette's cubicle, Liz came in with a serious attitude. I had never seen her look so pissed, and she didn't even speak to any of us. She went straight into her office and closed the door. I wondered what her attitude was all about, and just so she wouldn't come out and say anything to us, we all returned to our desks. I got busy stuffing some envelopes that needed to be mailed, and I heard Claudette on the phone with Korey, asking if he was coming to take her to lunch. I heard her give him a time, so I suspected that he'd be showing up soon.

Around ten o'clock, Liz came out of her office and came up to me. She put a piece of paper in front of me and asked me to look at it.

"What's wrong with this letter?" she asked.

Bitch, I don't know, you tell me, I thought. I looked it over, but didn't see anything. "I'm not sure. What's wrong with it?"

"The word 'tilted' should be 'titled.' I hope this letter didn't go out as is."

This was the first, maybe second, time something like that had happened. I always asked Liz to double check my work, and if she didn't do it, it was her own fault. "I put that letter on your desk for you to proof-read it. It hasn't gone out yet. I rarely make mistakes, Liz, and I apologize for the misspelled word."

Liz sighed, and asked me to come into her office. I did, and she told me to close the door behind her. "Have a seat," she said.

I eased into the chair, a bit nervous about her demeanor.

"Look, I apologize for snapping at you like that, but Mr. Aimes is driving me crazy. He's been on me about the refrigeration business being at a standstill, but people are just not buying appliances. I have to come up with a better marketing plan, and I'm going to be busy seeing what I can come up with. If you notice my door closed, don't let anyone disturb me. I have to get this done, because if production gets too slow, I don't have a job. You know what I mean by that, don't you?"

"I know exactly what you mean. And if you don't have one, I don't have one."

She chuckled and nodded. "You're right. So, you see how important this is to me. No interruptions, please."

"What if your husband calls? Do you want me to send his calls to you, or have him call you back?"

She threw her hand back and cut her eyes. "Don't send his calls in here either. Our anniversary was Friday night, and do you know his tail forgot about it? He'd rather work than celebrate our twenty-six years together. Where in the hell were his priorities?"

I wasn't sure about his priorities, but I surely knew where his fat dick was. It was being eased in and out of me, but I couldn't say that to Liz, could I? I'd had no idea it was their anniversary, but I was fucking flattered that Steven had set aside that day for me. I suspected that he and Liz had spent the weekend arguing, and if she kept up with this attitude, I knew he'd be calling me soon.

"If anybody wants to come through that door," I said, "they have to get by me. Go ahead and do what you have to do, and if I can help you with anything, please let me know. You know I don't mind. We have to look out for each other."

"Thank you," Liz said. "I don't know what I'd do without you."

I left Liz's office, keeping it off limits. When Claudette tried to go in there and bug her, I stopped her.

"She said no one, Claudette. She doesn't want to be bothered by anyone."

"But I need her to sign off on something. She wasn't referring to me when she said no one."

There was no doubt in my mind that she rode the special school bus to school. See, this is why I couldn't leave Korey alone. I wanted to get her where it hurt, and there were so many times that I'd thought about shanking her ass to shut her up. I rushed out of my seat, and stood in front of Liz's door.

"I said no, Claudette. Put the paper in my inbox marked 'signatures,' and Liz will sign off on those papers when she comes out of her office. I made her a promise, and I intend to keep it."

"Promise or not, she needs to sign this right away, for your information," she snapped. "I have to mail this out before the end of the day. If I don't, she's going to be mad at me, so move!"

I was just about to wrap my hands around that heifer's neck, but Liz opened her door. Veronica stood to look over her cubicle. The whole scene was quite embarrassing.

"What is going on out here?" Liz asked, removing her Kawasaki 704 series glasses like Sarah Palin. "I'm trying to get some work done."

Claudette reached over my shoulder and handed Liz the paper. "I didn't mean to disturb you, but I need your signature on this. You told me that needed to get mailed today, but Chase wouldn't let me knock on your door to give it to you."

Liz looked at the paper, then went to her desk and scribbled her signature. "This could have waited, Claudette, and please do not disturb me again. Chase is just doing a job that I asked her to do."

Liz gave the paper back to Claudette and shut her door. Yes, she got her paper signed, but her face was cracked because Liz took my side, not hers. Claudette looked over her cubicle at me, rolling her eyes. I called her a stupid bitch under my breath, but said it loud enough for her to hear it.

"What did you say?" she asked. "Did you say something to me?"

How about I'm screwing your man? I thought. Well. Lord knows if I ever felt like going there with her, I would have done it today. I had to calm myself, as losing my job was something I didn't want to do. Veronica entered my cubicle, trying to calm me. She had seen me in rare form, and did her best to prevent me from going there.

"Ignore her," she whispered. "Let's go take a break, Chase, and let things cool down."

Thank God Veronica came up with Plan B, because mine would have had me subjected to immediate termination. "That sounds like a good idea to me," I said to Veronica.

I got up from my chair, and followed Veronica outside. She was a smoker, so we stood outside the door of the building, talking. It was a bit chilly outside, but the chill was allowing me to cool off.

"I could tell you were about to slap her," Veronica said. "And who does she think she is, trying to bust into Liz's office like that?"

"The Queen of England, I guess. Liz told her butt, though, didn't she?"

"Yes. I was over there cracking up. I haven't forgotten how Claudette laughed underneath her breath at Tony going off on me at the Christmas party, and I've had some ill feelings about her ever since. Her man, Korey, got her so damn spoiled. Since she got him wrapped around her little finger, she think everybody else is supposed to jump when she tells them to."

"Girl, please. She don't have Korey wrapped anywhere, and if she did, he damn sure wouldn't be having sex with me."

I knew the moment those words left my mouth, they shouldn't have. I was beginning to trust Veronica, though, and like me, she really didn't like Claudette. Still, I had been so good at keeping my business a secret that it's a shame I let something like that slip. Veronica hadn't released the smoke from her Virginia Slims that she had sucked into her mouth, and when she did, the smoke came out quickly. "What in the hell did you just say?" she shouted.

"Nothing," I said. "I meant to say something else."

"Stop lying," she laughed. "I swear to God that Tony said that shit after the Christmas party that night. He mentioned the way Korey kept looking at you, and I told him he was a drunk fool who was just speculating about people he knew nothing about. Then, when we went to lunch that day, Claudette started talking about how she thought Korey was cheating on her. The look on your face had me thinking, but I was like no, this is not happening. Girl!" Veronica shouted. "Is it good? He is fine as hell and if he let me, I'd screw him too."

I placed my finger over my lips. Veronica was too loud. She was excited to find out more. "Aw, he's good. But, let's just say, not good enough."

"When is the last time y'all hooked up? I mean, is this an ongoing thing, and is he really going to marry that big-lip hoochie?"

"As far as I know, he's been going back and forth on it. They're having lunch today, so I assume he should be here in a little bit. I talk to him almost every single night, and the last time we hooked up was the week before last. Whatever you do, please, please don't say anything to anyone, Veronica. You owe me this favor, and if the word gets out, I don't want any trouble. You know what I mean?"

"I'm not saying one word. I'm just in shock, and as much as she brags about Korey, please. Some men will screw your mama, and they don't have no shame in their game."

"Exactly," I agreed.

We stayed outside for a few more minutes, continuing to talk. When I saw Korey's car pull into a parking spot, I warned Veronica not to look suspicious. She pretended to carry on a heavy conversation with me, and when Korey got near, he didn't say one word to us. He walked into the building, and just as Veronica was about to open her mouth, he stuck his head out the door.

"Say," he said to me, "ain't your name Chase?"

I nodded.

"You work with Claudette, right?"

I nodded again.

"I wanted to do something special for her, and I wondered if I could talk to you about it. Do you have a minute?"

"Sure," I said, excusing myself from Veronica. I could tell she wanted to crack up, but she maintained her composure, telling me she'd see me inside.

I followed Korey to the closed-in stairway and he sat on the steps. He placed his elbows on his knees and cracked his knuckles.

"What's up with you, ma? You've been putting me off, and you know what I've been asking you about. You haven't said one word to me about your decision, and quite frankly, I'm getting tired of waiting."

"Too bad, Korey, because I will put you off for as long as I want to. According to Claudette, the two of you are getting closer, and the lovemaking session last night was one to remember. You haven't forgotten about it already, have you?"

He slightly pursed his lips and leaned back on the stairs with his elbows behind him. I guess he hadn't counted on Claudette putting their business out there like she was.

"I'm not talking about all that. I'm talking about you and me. What's up with us, Chase? You're not going to have me dangling on this string for long. I'm about to cut it."

My brows rose. I damn sure wasn't having a good day. This fool and his woman were crazy. They deserved each other. "No, let me cut it for you. How dare you sit there and try to force me into a relationship when you're engaged. Every single day, I have to listen to your soon-to-be wife talk about you and her. You tell me one thing, but when Claudette comes in, she says another.

"Just who are you, Korey? Who or what do you really want? I don't know the answer to that question, so therefore, you will not get a decision from me as to how I anticipate us moving forward. You're lucky that I'm still messing with you, and the only reason I'm still doing that is for my own personal pleasures."

I pulled on the door, but Korey reached out to grab my hand. He shut the door, and held my hand with his.

"Calm down, all right? Listen, I told you that I would end it with Claudette if you wanted me to. That would be no problem for me, but you act like you don't want me to do it. Then you sit here and say what you said, and honestly, Chase, I'm the one confused. Tell me now: do you want me to end it or not? I'll go upstairs and do it right now. That's just how serious I am about us, but I'm not going to continue to be with you under your terms and conditions. I've played by your rules long enough, and your rules don't work for me anymore."

As much as I would have loved to see Korey bust Claudette's bubble right now, I didn't like his attitude. If the sex was over, cool. I'd get that elsewhere, so unfortunately, I had to set the record straight. "If you're done playing by my rules, then I guess our playtime is over. Good luck to you, Korey, and I do wish you and Claudette all the best. I guess I'll see you at the wedding."

He stood stone-faced for a moment, then reached for the door and walked out. These men were killing the hell out of me, and what other choice did I really have?

Chapter 7

You know the saying "you never really miss a good thing until it's gone"? Well, that applied to dick too. My well had run dry, simply because I had cut off Korey for basically becoming too obsessive. Steven and I had not seen each other since his anniversary. He hadn't called me, and I was never the kind of woman to go chasing after a man. I guess he figured I would call him, but that wasn't going to happen anytime soon. Even at work, he hadn't called the office to speak to Liz or anything. She'd been very busy with her marketing project, so I suspected that she'd already told him not to call unless it was important.

That seemed to be the difference with younger versus older men. The younger ones got wrapped too easily, but the older ones you had to slowly manipulate into doing what you wanted. I had so many tricks up my sleeves for Steven, but we had to get to a point where sex between us was more frequent. We hadn't gotten to that point yet. I suspected that he was feeling a bit guilty about what he'd done; after all, it was on his anniversary. What I did know, though, was that he'd soon get over his guilty feeling and realize that I was just a phone call away.

According to Claudette, the wedding was still on. And as the days ticked away, excitement grew in her eyes. She had already apologized to me about our disagreement, and I apologized to her as well. It didn't dawn on me that the only reason she wanted to settle our differences was so that I'd be sure to come to her wedding. She bragged about how much her parents had spent, and claimed that it was going to be the event of the year. I was so sure that it was, and since I hadn't heard from Korey, I suspected that he'd made his mind up about what to do. I kept my fingers crossed for them, in hopes that he would be the man only she envisioned him to be.

Claudette had taken the entire week off from work, and it was so peaceful and quiet. Her wedding was on Saturday, and instead of it being at a church, it was at a hall her parents had rented. The reception was to follow on the lower level, and I couldn't wait to see the place. Claudette made it sound like a palace, but Veronica said that one of her friends got married at the same place. She described it as being "nice" and said that Claudette's description was overboard.

Either way, I stood by the door with my sky blue dress on, waiting for Veronica to pick me up. My bun and bangs had been working for me so well that I opted to keep my hair as it was. The dress was simple, but any dress that I wore always looked sexy because of my curves. I went with a pearl necklace and earrings, and even wore a bangle of pearls around my wrist. I played it conservative, knowing that Liz would be there, possibly with Steven. I couldn't wait to see him again, nor could I wait to see Korey's reaction.

I figured this would be a very tough day for him to get through, but then again, a man definitely knew how to play his game. He pretended to be so unhappy around me, and all he talked about was how he and Claudette were growing away from each other. When it was all said and done, he wasn't too unhappy. The wedding was on, and he had plenty of opportunities to stop it if he wanted to.

Veronica called, telling me that she was outside waiting. I rushed outside, only to bump into Lance on my way to Veronica's car. He caught me off guard, grabbing me into his arms and hugging my waist.

"Play along with me," he whispered, shifting his eyes from side to side. I figured one of his women was somewhere looking on.

"What . . . Who is it?" I mumbled underneath my breath.

He laughed and kissed my cheek. "I'm just kidding. You look nice, though. Have fun wherever you're going."

I playfully slapped his arm and he headed up the steps. When I got inside Veronica's car, she couldn't help but ask what that was all about.

"Girl, Lance always be playing with me like that. He is so crazy."

"He likes you, though. That's why he didn't want to take me on a date."

"He didn't say that, Veronica. I told you he just said he was interested in somebody else and didn't want to involve you in his mess. Between you and me, it be a gang of women at his apartment. When one woman leaves out the back, another one comes through the front."

"Dang. He doing it like that? He don't seem like the type, but he is rather sexy."

I had gotten to a point where I thought he was too, but I kept quiet. No doubt, Lance was growing on me.

Veronica and I arrived at the wedding almost forty-five minutes early. It was already packed, and to be honest with you, the hall was decorated really prettily. Claudette's colors were pink, black, white, and a hint of silver. White chairs filled the hall and pink bows were on the back of each chair. Silver and black decorations were throughout and the flower arrangements were beautiful. The lighting was dim, but not too dim where you couldn't see. Almost every chair was filled, but when Veronica spotted Liz, she waved at us. She had reserved two seats for us, and my heart sank to my stomach when I saw Steven sitting next to her. My mind shot back to that night in his office, and I wondered if he was or had been thinking about it too.

I followed Veronica, hoping that she wouldn't take the seat directly next to Steven. She stopped to give Liz a hug, and shook Steven's hand as she passed by him. I hugged Liz too, and when I reached for Steven's hand he gripped it hard.

"Hello, Chase, how are you?"

"I'm doing well, and you?"

"Couldn't be better."

Since Liz wasn't paying attention, I gave him a quick wink, hoping that Veronica wouldn't sit next to him. Thank God she didn't, and she left the seat right next to him for me. Liz looked sharp as ever, and the sheer, flowing mustard and brown dress she wore couldn't be duplicated. She accessorized her outfit with gold, and the pretty rings on her fingers looked as if they cost a fortune. Her wedding ring was glistening too.

"This hall is beautiful, isn't it?" she whispered, looking past Steven to talk to me and Veronica.

We both agreed that it was, and as we continued to talk, I noticed just how uncomfortable Steven was. Every once in a while, he looked at me through his peripheral vision, but he wouldn't turn his head. I noticed him suck his teeth a few times, and when he rubbed his beard, I wondered what was on his mind. This was definitely an awkward feeling, and it was too bad that I was making him so uncomfortable. I was ready for the wedding to get started; maybe that would settle things down a bit.

I was talking to Veronica about the expensive-looking chandeliers hanging from up above, and felt someone tap my shoulder.

"Excuse me," the young man said. "You're wanted out in the hallway."

I pointed to myself, thinking that the young man had tapped the wrong person. "Who, me?"

"Yes. Follow me. Please."

I wasn't sure what this was about, and I knew Claudette hadn't asked anyone to come get me to help her. When I got into the hallway, an older man was standing there waiting for me. He had on a tuxedo, so I suspected that he was part of the wedding party. He told the younger man to go into another room.

"Go ahead and finish getting ready," he said to the younger man. "And tell everyone that we have less than forty-five minutes to go." He looked at me. "As for you, young lady, please follow me."

I wasn't used to taking orders, so I didn't move. "Where are we going and who sent for me?"

"I'm not supposed to say, but from what he says, seeing you is very important."

I wasn't too thrilled about what was going on, as I really didn't know who any of these people were. When we got to the lower level, the man opened the door to a spacious room. I followed him inside, and saw Korey dressed in his tuxedo, sitting in a folding silver chair. Mirrors were around the room, and two tuxedos were sitting on the table next to him.

"Thanks, man," he said to the older gentleman. "And make sure you close the door on your way out."

"Got it."

The man left the room, closing the door behind him as he was told. I turned to Korey, who looked dynamite in his tuxedo. His skin was smooth as ever, and his wavy hair was cut with a deep, fresh lining.

"So, I guess you're going to let me go through with this, huh?" he asked.

"This has nothing to do with me, Korey, and you have to do what feels right for you. No matter what, you need to be honest with yourself, but if you're having doubts about this, why are you here? I can't believe that you've gone this many months without telling Claudette how you really feel. As much as I don't care for her, you are wrong for keeping your true feelings inside. Again, don't make this about me, because I already told you where I stand on this."

He stood up and put his hands in his pockets. He started to pace the floor and looked down at it. "So, where do you stand, Chase? Have you been thinking about me or not? If I get married, can I still play by your rules or have you shut out that opportunity as well?"

"Yes, I've been thinking about you, but maybe not in a way that you want me to. This connection that you keep talking about between us is very sexual, and to be honest with you, that's all it is. If you're looking for someone to cook every day for you, clean your house, have your children, and wash your back for you when you get home from work, I'm not the woman for you. I don't envision that kind of life with any man right now, so do not take what I'm saying to you personally."

Korey stood for a moment to look at me, then shook his head. "How in the hell did I get myself so caught up with you? I knew this would go down like this, so if you want to make this all about sex with us, then so be it." He looked at his watch and removed his bowtie. "I got twenty minutes before show time. Take off your clothes."

I took a few steps back. "What? Are you crazy? I'm not taking off my clothes."

I turned to walk toward the door, and Korey came after me. He took my hand, and hit the light switch next to the wall, putting us in pure darkness.

"Five, ten minutes is all I ask. I need to get into you before I do this, and please don't deny me. If you won't let me have you in the way that I want you, at least allow me a few minutes of satisfaction with you before I get married."

I couldn't believe I was standing there even considering this. This would no doubt go down in my little black book as trifling. Thing was, I loved spontaneous and risky sex, and the moment seemed so perfect. By now, Korey's hands were already squeezing my inner thighs and touching my slit through the crotch of my silk panties. I wanted to make it quick, so I stepped out of my panties and pulled my dress up over my hips. Korey turned the lights back on, claiming that he wanted to see what was about to go down. He rushed to put a condom on, and as he lay back on one of the seat benches, I straddled his lap, allowing my feet to touch the floor. His tuxedo pants were only lowered to his knees, but that was no problem for me. I started to ride him, using the floor for leverage as I moved up and down. My legs muscles were being put to work, but it was all so worth it. Korey hadn't been inside of me in a minute, and the feel of him brought back memories of what I had been missing. We both moaned and groaned, but did our best to keep our voices low so no one would hear us. Time was not on our side, and as we rocked our bodies together for fifteen long minutes, we finally came at the same time. I leaned forward to give him one last juicy and wet long kiss, then removed myself from on top of him. He continued to lay flat on the bench, but his eyes were closed while he rested his arm on his forehead.

"Thank you," he said. "I needed that."

I picked up my panties from the floor, tossing them in the trash. My hand touched the doorknob to exit. "I enjoyed myself too. Now, get up and go do you. I'm sure your beautiful bride is waiting."

I left the room, quickly searching for a restroom so I could tidy myself up. I did, and afterward, I hurried to find my seat. Veronica and Liz asked where I had gone, but I told them that I had to go outside to make an important phone call. I mentioned that it was something about my ill father, lying my butt off.

"Yeah, right," Veronica said. "I don't believe—"

I nudged her waist and whispered, "We'll talk later."

Besides that, the spicy aroma of sex was still coming from between my legs, and the way Steven was eye-balling me, I wasn't sure if he suspected something. I crossed my legs, attempting to tone down the smell.

A few minutes later the wedding got started. I was doing okay, until I saw Korey and his groomsmen come into the room. He did not have a smile on his face, and his eyes searched the room. They stopped as soon as they got to me, and I quickly turned my head in Veronica's direction. She nudged my side again, but I shifted my eyes away from her too. Just so I didn't have to look at Korey, I dropped my head and softly massaged my forehead. I was starting to get a headache, and when the wedding party started coming down the aisle, I put on a fake smile.

"They are too cute," Liz said about the flower girl and ring bearer. I agreed, and when Steven finally looked into my eyes, I was caught in a trance. If I weren't already so sticky and wet between my legs, I would have hiked my dress up again. He finally blinked and looked away, right before the moment of truth came. "Here Comes the Bride" played, and everyone stood. The double doors in the back opened, and Claudette stepped into the room, looking prettier than I had ever seen her.

Even her lips didn't look as big, and her hair was pinned up on top of her head. The dress she had on looked like it was embedded with tiny diamonds, and it had a flaring tail at the bottom. No wonder she was anxious for all of us to come to her wedding, because there would have been no way for her to brag about this without us seeing it. We definitely had to see for ourselves. Liz was all smiles, and so was everyone else. When I looked at Korey, though, he held his hands together in front of him, but there was no expression on his face whatsoever. His eyes were glued on Claudette, and I was relieved that they weren't on me. She made it to the front, and everyone took their seats. Korey stepped beside her, and they both faced the minister.

He gave his spiel about who gives this woman, and her father stated, "I do." The ceremony continued, and since they had prepared their own vows, Claudette was asked to go first. She took Korey's hand and smiled as she looked into his eyes. The same blank expression was on his face.

"Korey, from the first day I met you, I knew that we would someday be standing here. Being with you has given me so much joy, and I can't wait to spend the rest of my life with you as your loving wife. I promise to always remain faithful, loving and supportive of you, and because of the man you have always presented yourself to be, you truly deserve it. I love you with everything that there is in me, and I look forward to making you one of the happiest men in the entire world."

Oh, my, God, I sat there thinking. How in the hell would he offer a comeback to something like that? The guilt from what we had done was already eating me alive, and I really didn't even like Claudette. I could only imagine what Korey was feeling, and when I saw his eyes water, my stomach started to rumble. He continued to hold Claudette's hand, but before he spoke, he played it off and wiggled his finger underneath his right eye like something was in it. He blinked to clear the water from his eyes, then took in a deep breath, slowly releasing it.

"Claudette, you have truly been too good to me. Thing is, I am not deserving of your love, nor have I ever been." I sat up straight, holding my stomach with anticipation of his next words. "I brought you here today, and made you go through all of this, knowing deep inside that I did not want this. I'm so sorry, baby, but I'm not in love with you anymore."

Everybody was in complete and utter shock. In a few seconds, pandemonium was about to erupt, and no sooner than I thought it, it did.

"Oh no, he didn't," one lady shouted.

"Shame! Shame on you," said another older lady standing with a cane.

"Son of a B!" a man shouted at Korey as he started walking down the aisle. When his eyes connected with mine, I prayed to God that he wouldn't come over to me. He didn't, and as he was walking out the door, Claudette and her father were yelling his name. Another woman had stormed after him, and I assumed since she looked like Claudette, she was her mother. Her face was beet red and her tightened fists were in the air.

"You lousy motherfucker," she shouted, going after him. "How could you do this to my daughter!"

Claudette started crying in her father's arms, and her grandmother stood up, thanking everyone for coming.

"It looks like there will be no wedding today, so thank you all for taking time out of your busy schedules to be here. We ask that you leave now so the family can deal with this alone."

Many of us were still sitting there in shock, trying to figure out what in the hell had happened. Veronica kept nudging my side, but I was too afraid to face her. Steven looked at me again, and then turned to Liz. He stood up, and held out his hand so she could take it.

"Are you ready to go? Obviously, there's not going to be a wedding, so let's go."

Liz took his hand and slowly stood. "I wonder what happened?" She continued to look at Claudette being comforted by her father. "I hope she'll be okay."

"It's clear that the young man had a change of heart. I'm sure she'll get over it," Steven said.

Liz's brows rose higher, and the look she gave Steven was devious. "That's not nice to say. He shouldn't have done that. What a hurtful thing to do to her."

"You have no idea what was going on with the two of them. You're on the outside looking in. Hurtful or not, at least he was smart enough not to go through with it. You've got to give him credit for that." Steven wasn't backing down, and that's what I liked about him. A man who spoke his mind was all right with me.

Liz was so disgusted that she walked away from him. As we exited our row, Steven was close behind me. So close, that I felt *something* touch my backside.

"Excuse me," he said as we stepped out of our row. "I didn't mean to bump you."

"No problem," I said. "Just make it up to me later."

Steven winked and left to go find his upset wife.

Veronica, however, saw the entire exchange.

"What did you mean when you asked him to make it up to you later? Make what up to you?"

"I didn't say that," I lied. "I said, 'Tell Liz to call me later.'"

"You need to stop your lying," she said as we exited the hall. "I heard what you said, and I can't believe you said that to him. What if he tells Liz you said that to him?"

"He won't, trust me."

"Why not?"

"Because he has every reason not to say a word to her, that's why."

Veronica was trying to put two and two together, and she had forgotten about all of the drama that had happened inside. "Girl, please don't tell me that you're doing it with Mr. Smith too. I'm going to drop dead if something is going on with the two of you as well."

I hated to go there, but it felt good for me to get this off my chest. "I hope you got your casket already picked out, because it is what it is."

Veronica playfully dropped to the ground, and the people around us asked if she was okay. "I'm fine," she said, slowly getting up. "You and I are going to your apartment right now to talk! I need to know why you disappeared at the wedding, and about you and Mr. Smith. I definitely didn't see that one coming, but all I can say is, you are one happy-go-lucky dog!"

I knew Veronica would understand, and yet again, I made her promise to keep my secret. For whatever reason, I trusted that she would.

Chapter 8

After the funeral—wedding—was over, I thought I'd be able to breathe a little, especially since Claudette would be off for the following week from work. I had no time to do anything, as Liz was on my back, ordering me around and expecting me to do everything. All I could say was that you sure could tell when there was trouble in paradise. Liz's attitude had changed, and I knew it wasn't all about her issues with Mr. Aimes. The way she and Steven had snapped at each other at the wedding, it was obvious that they had issues with each other. Liz wasn't like Claudette, though. She had never been around here running her mouth about her husband. She didn't have pictures all over the place, but I was so lucky that she brought him to the Christmas party. I still hadn't heard from him, and after our little exchange at the funeral—sorry, wedding—I thought he would have called. I was very anxious to hook up with him again, and if he hadn't called me by Thursday, I was going to check in.

Other than that, Korey had called to thank me for

helping him see the light. He was interrupting *Wheel of Fortune*, so I was tuning in and out of the conversation.

"You weren't the only person I was seeing, Chase, and my life was spiraling out of control. I felt bad about what I had to do at the wedding, but I actually did Claudette a huge favor. She doesn't see it now, but one day she'll understand. Meanwhile, where does that leave us?"

"It leaves us out on a limb, because you haven't learned yet how to play by my rules."

"It's hard playing by your rules, only because I want so much more from you. I have some major thinking to do, and if I think this can work out for me, I'll be in touch." He hung up, and all I thought was *Whatever!*

Korey was too confused for me, and he turned me off by not standing up for himself sooner. If you didn't want to be with somebody, just tell her. How simple was that? That's what irritated me about most men. They never knew how to come clean, and always preferred to play these games that hurt too many feelings. Many women could accept the truth, but the thing was, the truth was rarely being told. By all means, I wasn't an expert or anything like that, but I could respect a man who was honest with me, and one who didn't keep secrets about his on-the-side relationships. Give me a chance to decide if I want to deal with you, but don't be wining and dining me, and telling me I'm the only one when I'm not. That was bull, and in this day and age, that kind of mess was getting played out. Some women like myself were beginning to catch on, and if a man wasn't willing to present to me who he really was, then he was basically wasting his time.

* * *

While I was at work on Wednesday, I had gotten a call from the nursing home in Norfolk, Virginia, telling me my father had passed away. He wanted to be cremated, and his girlfriend of eight years was ordered to do whatever she wished with his ashes. I wanted to force myself to cry, but why waste my tears? I had made peace with my father, and it was because of him that I couldn't connect with men like I wanted to. I had even gone to counseling about what he'd done to me, but the counselor assured me that in time I would heal. I wasn't sure if I had gotten to that healing point or not.

I sat at my desk, biting my nails as I thought about my father's middle-of-the-night visits. I could never get the thought out of my mind of his sweaty body on top of me and the pain I felt from him ripping my insides apart. Thinking of that, yes, I had to wipe a tear that had fallen down my face. I wished the molestation had never happened, and I often wondered if I would have turned out to be a different person. My father often asked me if I loved him, and told me that if I did, I had to do certain things to prove it. The molestation started when I was nine years old and lasted until I was fourteen. By then, I hated him with a passion, and I knew wrong from right. It was because of him that I'd had relationship issues. I tried giving a man my all, but it never worked out for me. I kept finding myself being caught up with no-good men, and I wasn't tolerant of the drama that came along with them. It was funny how women my age were thinking about when they'd get married and were planning to have children. All I was thinking about was taking care of me, and hooking up with a man who could give me the best pleasure he possibly could. I didn't know if I would always feel this way, but for now, it was working for me just fine.

I left work on Wednesday, and instead of waiting until tomorrow, I had to go see what was up with Steven. First, I called his office to see if he was there. His secretary said that he was in a meeting, but would be wrapping it up shortly. I hurried to his office, not knowing if he would leave. When I got there, he was standing in the lobby, shaking hands with two other men. They walked away and I stepped up to him.

"Do you have a minute?" I asked.

Without saying a word, he turned and I followed him to his office. He closed the door and offered me a seat. I chose the one in front of his desk, crossing my legs in front of me. He sat behind his desk, looking a bit stiff.

"What brings you by?" he asked.

"I was getting worried. I haven't heard from you and I thought I'd hear from you soon."

"As you can see," he said, looking down at the stacks of papers on his desk, "I've been a busy man."

"All work and no play, huh? You shouldn't deprive yourself like that, and I was so sure that you wouldn't."

"I don't intend to for long. I had planned to call you, but some things have been on my mind lately."

"Things like what?"

He sat back in his chair, tracing his trimmed beard with his fingers. "Are you involved with, uh, what's his face . . . Claudette's man? You know, the one who left her at the altar."

I was stunned that he mentioned it and wanted to know why. "Why do you ask?"

"Because I sensed it. I noticed it at the Christmas party and at the wedding. His eyes are always glued to you like a laser beam, and something is definitely up with that."

It amazed me how the men could catch on so quickly, but the women couldn't. We were the ones known for paying attention, but I guess not detailed attention. I figured Steven was waiting for me to lie, but I had no problem being up front about the situation, especially to someone I wanted to involve myself with. "We were involved, but not anymore."

"I see," he said, sitting up straight, rubbing his hands together. "So, let me get this straight. You've been fucking him, and I suspect, you want to continue fucking me too. You work with Claudette and Liz, knowing that this can come out in the open at any given time. I'm supposed to take this risk, right along with you, and take a chance on destroying my twenty-five years of marriage to Liz. Is that what you want me to do?"

I uncrossed my legs and leaned slightly forward. "In case you forgot, it's twenty-six years of marriage to Liz, not twenty-five. And I don't expect you to do anything that you're not willing to do. If you can't handle this, then I understand. I really thought you could, and for the record, no, I don't intend to keep fucking a boy when I can get pure pleasure from a man. If you aren't the one, forgive me, Steven, for being so very wrong about you."

He snickered. His look and body language were stern. "Listen, I can handle anything you bring my way, so don't underestimate me. I'm not your average Joe, and I can tell that you've been at this for a very long time. For the record, though, if any of this ever gets back to Liz, or anyone else in that office, things are going to get rough. Not for me, but for you. Don't get any ideas about me leaving my wife, because I sim-

ply will not do it. I'm already in love and I'm not looking to love again. I'm frugal with my money, so if
you're looking for a sugar daddy, you're definitely in
the wrong place. Last, but not least, do not come to my
office again, or call here. We can only hook up at hotels, or if you have a better place in mind, let me
know."

I stood and stepped up to Steven's desk. I rested my
palms on it, clearing my throat just to make sure my
tone was sharp. "You have no idea how much I appreciate a man who tells it like it is. And, for your records,
I have no love to give. I don't give a damn about your
wife, and if she ever finds out about us, too f-ing bad.
You will be way more hurt than I will, so you'd better
be 100 percent sure that this is something you, Mr.
Smith, can handle. As for your money, keep it, because
I already have enough. And if I want you to be my
sugar daddy, trust me, you will. For now, all I'm interested in is your big dick, and how you're going to
make sure that it delivers an immaculate performance
each and every time we get together. If it doesn't, that's
the only time you'll hear me gripe or complain. Because as soon as you fall short, I will drop you like a
hot potato and pretend that you never, ever existed.
Now, does that sound doable for you? If not, you let
me know."

Steven stood, then walked around his desk to stand
next to me. He put his hands in his pockets, while staring at me for brief moment. "You got trouble written
deep in your eyes. But you know what . . . you're so
fucking sexy that I'm willing to take my chances. I'm
going to put that hot pussy of yours on speed dial, and
I don't want you complaining like you were the last

time we got together. And if your performance starts to lack, I will dismiss you and go back to giving my wife my all. Meet me at the same hotel I mentioned before, tomorrow night at seven. Come prepared, and expect to stay with me all night. I told Liz I'd be out of town for the weekend, so I guess I'll see you tomorrow."

I moved in front of Steven, resting my arms on his shoulders. I pressed my body against his, just to get a rise. "Can't wait," I said, leaning in for a kiss. His kisses were always intense, and I rubbed the back of his head so he'd keep it coming. When his hands massaged my ass, I couldn't help but reach down and give him a massage too. I comforted his package, feeling how hard and thick it was.

"Are you sure you want to wait until tomorrow?" I asked. "What about tonight?"

"Tomorrow," he said. "That way we'll have much more time."

I agreed, and when a light knock was at the door, I backed away from him. He wiped his lips, and I followed him to see who it was. It was his secretary, telling him that she was wrapping it up for the day. He told her good night, then walked me to the exit as well.

As my mother always said, when you want something, pursue it. I did, and ten times out of ten, I got what I wanted, never settling for less. I spent the entire weekend shacked up with Steven at a hotel. No doubt, we did our thing, and it floored me how people reacted behind closed doors. Steven and I watched porn movies together, we got tipsy, and I enjoyed him taking Vodka shots from my belly button. When the alcohol seeped between my legs, he was there to sip it up. We couldn't get enough of each other, and when Sunday night rolled around, I was beat.

My coochie was tender from the beating it had taken, and after sitting in the tub for at least an hour to cool myself, that didn't help. Maybe because Steven was in there with me, getting the last of our good-bye. I honestly liked him, and I could see this thing between us continuing for quite some time. He didn't mention Liz's name once, and even when she called, he didn't try to hide it. He spoke to her right in front of me, and expressed to her that he was having a decent time in Michigan. After returning the love over the phone, he dropped it on the bed and got back to entertaining me.

On Monday, I regretted that Claudette had made it back to work. She was so embarrassed, and could look no one in their eyes. Veronica and I couldn't help but go to her cubicle to see what was up.

"I'm not in the mood to talk right now," she snapped. "I have a lot of work to catch up on, so don't bug me."

Veronica growled at her like a tiger, and we couldn't help but laugh. "Go ahead and bite our heads off," Veronica said. "We don't care. I just came over here to cheer you up, but if you don't wish to be bothered, I understand."

Veronica walked away, and I followed suit. Claudette had been humiliated enough, so I left her alone. At least for the day.

Liz hadn't made it to the office yet, but when I got to my desk, she called.

"I'm a bit under the weather," she said. "I'll be in tomorrow. If anything urgent comes up, be sure to call me at home."

"Okay," I said. "I hope you feel better. See you to-morrow."

Since Liz rarely took time off from work, I used this opportunity to sit around and do nothing. I needed this time, especially so I could reminisce about my weekend with Steven. He was already starting to get comfortable with me, and that was such good news for me. As I was in thought, I heard a familiar voice and looked up. Korey was standing in front of Claudette's cubicle, looking mad as hell.

"Why'd you do that shit?" he yelled at her. "You didn't have to run up my credit cards like that, and you are going to pay back every single penny. As for my car, that was cool too. My deductible is one thousand dollars and I'm here to collect."

"What are you talking about?" Claudette softly said. "I have no clue why you're here. I did nothing with your credit cards or to your car. If you don't leave, right now, I will call security and have you arrested."

"I don't give a damn, Claudette. You need to grow the hell up and stop playing these childish games. That's why I left you at the wedding looking stupid. I'm so glad that I didn't marry you."

She jumped up and wiggled her finger in his face. "Not as glad as I am. Now, get out of here and don't come to my job again."

Everybody was on their feet, looking over their cubicles and trying to see what was going on. I was so glad that Korey hadn't said anything about us, and when he looked at me before walking away, I thought it was a wrap. Unfortunately, he kicked in his Plan B. And just as I sighed from relief, he came back and entered Claudette's cubicle again. He removed his ring from his pocket, and dropped it on her desk. "By the way, I

forgot to give that bullshit back to you. If you wouldn't
mind giving me back the ring that I got you, so I can
pay for this stupid shit you did, I'd appreciate it."

Claudette rolled her neck around, while she remained in her seat. "I'm not giving you nothing back!
You can kiss my tail, Korey, and kiss that ring good-
bye because I already sold that sucker on eBay."

He leaned in close to her, going in on the attack. "If
you had an ass, maybe I would kiss it. Or maybe I
wouldn't have had to stick my dick in women with a
much better ass than yours, including that sexy-ass
coworker of yours that you always tell me how much
you despise. Yeah, you know the one, don't you? And if
you didn't know by now that being inside of her pussy
is the reason I couldn't get with yours, now you know."

I stood frozen in time. My jaw had already dropped,
and if you looked close enough, you could see steam
coming from my ears. No, Korey didn't just go there!
Even though his words weren't loud enough for everyone to hear, I heard them and so did Veronica. Claudette had definitely heard them, but before she could
get up out of her seat to go after Korey, he jetted. She
immediately turned to me, eyes cold as ever. There
was a way out of this, but I wasn't completely sure
what it was.

She gritted her teeth and a tear rolled down her face.
"I hope to God that what he said wasn't true."

My face was all scrunched, and I pointed to my chest.
"Who, me?" I said. "You despise me? I didn't know you
felt that way about me, Claudette, and I am stunned."

"Don't play games with me," she yelled as if she had
some authority. "Were you having sex with my fiancé?"

Now, I was trying to keep everything on the down
low, but Claudette was making a scene. Veronica had

even gone over to her cubicle to calm her, but she snatched away from her.

"Leave me the hell alone," she said to Veronica. "This bitch needs to answer my question. Did you, or didn't you?"

That just about did it for me, and calm as ever, I let Claudette have it. "Yes. And I'm a bad bitch, too, Claudette. The kind who fucked your man ten minutes before he met you at the altar, with a dick still dripping wet from my juices. No wonder he couldn't go through with the wedding. I had been telling him all along to get rid of you. You are so stupid and that's what you get for putting all of your business out there in the workplace. You increased my appetite for your man, and now you're mad because I couldn't help myself. Get a grip, bitch, and go somewhere and sit down."

She tried to rush around her cubicle and into mine. Veronica held her back, and when a supervisor from another department came over, they did their best to restrain her. I already had the phone in my hand, calling security. I wasn't about to go to jail today for knocking Claudette on her ass. And if she didn't stop calling me out of my name, I may have had to change my mind.

"You are such a conniving slut! I knew there was something about you that I didn't like. You and Korey deserve each other! Go to hell, Chase, and take him to hell with you!"

Claudette made herself look like a crazed woman who was in dire need of a straight jacket. When security got there, they had to haul her butt out of there by her arms. She was yelling and screaming, acting a complete fool. All over a man, I might add, who really and truly wasn't worth it. I wasn't even going to call and confront Korey about what he'd done. He knew he didn't have to go that far, and I guessed he was saying to hell with me, as I had said to hell with him.

I wasn't sure what was going to happen to Claudette. Everybody was stopping by, asking what had gone on between us. Veronica was telling only half of the story, but many had heard that I'd been having sex with Claudette's man. Some of the women looked at me with disgust, but there were others who laughed about it and wanted details. I kept my mouth shut, but as soon as I saw Liz, I knew there would be trouble. She looked tired as ever, and had bags underneath her eyes.

"Step into my office," she said to me.

I went into her office, closing the door behind me. Liz plopped into her seat and closed her eyes as she massaged the back of her neck. She sneezed, then reached for a napkin to wipe her red nose.

"What in the hell happened here today? I got a phone call from another supervisor, telling me that you and Claudette had been fighting."

I sat in the chair, preparing myself to tell the truth. "We weren't fighting, and whoever told you that wasn't being truthful. Korey came up here, yelling at Claudette about her running up his credit cards and causing some kind of damage to his car. They were arguing, and he mentioned to her that he'd had sex with me. She went ballistic and started calling me all kinds of names and threatening me. I called security and they came and got her."

Liz sniffled and rubbed her throat. "Were you really having sex with her fiancé?"

"Yes."

Liz cut her eyes and shook her head. "Then what did you expect her to do, Chase? Claudette has been going through hell these past few weeks, and you should have known better than to involve yourself with her fiancé. Excuse my French, but what kind of shit is that? Are you out of your mind?"

"Liz, I don't mean to be rude or anything, but you are weighing in on a situation that you know nothing about. I really don't have to discuss my personal business with you, but if you must know, I am the kind of woman who has no problem going after what I want, especially when it comes to men."

"There have to be limitations. You can't go after any man, especially if he's involved with someone in your family, workplace, or if he's married. I can't tell you how upset I would be if it were my husband, but thank God that he has enough sense to ignore women with your mentality. I don't even understand how a man like Korey got trapped, but—"

"If you don't understand, Liz, then I suggest you open your eyes a little wider and stop giving men credit where credit isn't due. As for your husband, don't thank God too soon, as one day you may find yourself in a messed-up situation, wondering why or how you got there. It's happened to me before, and you are in no way exempt. The bottom line here is, Korey was not in love with Claudette and that is why he didn't marry her. I'm sorry if she manipulated you into believing that her relationship was all that, but the truth of the matter is, their relationship had problems and not solely because of me."

Liz slammed her hand on her desk. "Why?" she

yelled. "Why do we as women keep on doing this shit to ourselves! We all chase after one freaking man, always giving him whatever it is that he wants. Have some damn dignity for yourself, Chase, and be smart enough to recognize when you're being used. And if a man is involved with someone else, then leave him the hell alone! Is it that hard to reject these jerks and tell them no, you're not that kind of woman?"

Pertaining to her husband, it was very hard. I could only imagine what she would say or how she would feel if she ever found out about me and Steven. She was pissed about the whole thing, and Korey wasn't even her man.

"No, it's not that hard at all, but depending on who the person is, I might not wish to reject them. That's what happened in this case, and no matter what anyone says, my personal life is what it is. Up until now, it has not interfered with my work, and my only concern is what do you intend to do about this incident."

Liz sighed. "For now, there's not much that I can do. I am going to give Claudette a few days off to cool down, and if the two of you wish to continue to work here, there better not be any more instances like the one that happened today. It's going to be hard for you two to get along, but for the sake of keeping your jobs, you have to do it."

"So you're not going to fire her? After threatening me and carrying on like she did, she's not getting fired?"

"A warning, yes. Fired, no. Consider yourself warned too, and if this job ever gets too uncomfortable for you, Chase, you can seek employment elsewhere. Now, please return to your desk and get some kind of work done today. As for me, I'm going back home to my bed and to my husband."

Liz's words really shocked me. She had rarely thrown her husband into the mix, but maybe it was just me. Her attitude had been changing toward me a little, but maybe I was thinking so because my attitude was starting to change toward her.

Chapter 9

I had already started to look for another job. Being around Claudette was too uncomfortable for me, and the same went for Liz. I could tell she was upset with me, and the only person that I enjoyed being around was Veronica. We started to hang out a lot, and she'd either come to my apartment on the weekends or I'd go to her house. I was surprised about how well she'd kept it in order, and it was good to see how much her life had changed since she'd gotten rid of Tony. No doubt, Veronica was progressing, and she could have done so a long time ago if she had been willing to toss out her extra baggage.

The past weekend, we got together at Lance's place, and had a blast chilling with him and talking about all that was going on in his life, as well as mine. Lance and Veronica were down-to-earth people who weren't trying to judge anybody or their situations. That's why I couldn't get with Claudette, or, for that matter, Liz. They probably had never been through much of anything, and couldn't understand how a woman like me had turned out as I had. I couldn't care less what either of them thought of me, and as the weeks trickled by, Steven and I were getting closer and closer by the day. He had gotten to the point where he started to call my cell phone a lot. He was sort of checking in, and that was fine by me. I sat in the break room, far away from Liz and another supervisor, cheesing as I spoke to Steven on the phone. He'd just asked what color panties I had on.

"What color do you think?"

"Red?"

"Nope. I wore red yesterday."

"Black?"

"No, I'm sick of black. I have on a boring gray, but lacy."

"Sounds good to me. I wanted to, uh, see you tonight, but I won't be able to. I'm working late at the office, but I want you to go on a business trip with me next weekend. You think you can handle that?"

"Maybe. But if it's business, you won't have time to play with me, will you?"

"Baby, I'll make time. Just have your things ready and packed to go."

"Where are we going?"

"Where else but to Vegas. It'll be fun, and you know I'm all about that."

"You most certainly are. I'll chat with you later, and thanks for spicing up my boring day. I'm starting to really hate this place, and I'm so ready to find another job."

"I told you I'd help you find one, so quit pouting. You don't need to be in that office with Liz anyway. I'm still a bit uncomfortable with that."

"Why? 'Cause she be at home dogging me out, doesn't she? I know she does."

Steven laughed, and he didn't have to answer. "Let's just say that she's got some serious issues with you. Hang in there, though, and I'll see what I can do."

I flipped my phone shut, sure that Steven would get me out of this mess soon. I cut my eyes at Liz as she sat at the other table, running her mouth. I wondered what it was like for the two of them at home, and more than anything, I wanted to know if Steven was giving it to her like he was giving it to me.

Before I got back to work, I hurried into Liz's office and looked for her keys. Now, this wasn't about me stalking her or anything like that, but I just wanted to see how the man who was giving so much to me was reacting at home. Every mistress wanted to know these kinds of things. When I found Liz's keys in her drawer, I couldn't figure out which one was her house key. It was a toss-up between two of them, as the other two keys had the names of her vehicle maker on them. I quickly removed both keys, and hurried out to find a locksmith. One was right around the corner from where we worked, and when I got a duplicate of the keys, I rushed back to the office. Nosy-ass Claudette was at her desk, and she watched as I went inside of Liz's office to close the door. I quickly put the keys back on her key ring and left her office.

When five o'clock came, I was still working on a paper for Liz and hurried to finish up. She always worked way after five, so I figured she wasn't leaving anytime soon. Her door was closed, so I opened it and put the paper on her desk. She was on the phone, and mouthed the words "thank you" to me and waved. I nodded, and left to go handle my business for the evening.

I grabbed a quick bite to eat, then drove to the address that I had written on a piece of paper. As soon as I turned into the subdivision, my eyes were popping out of their sockets. There were some bad houses lined up on their street, and all of the houses sat on acres and acres of land. I looked at the address on the paper, and compared it to the brick-framed house in front of me. It was built like a castle, and had a four-car garage and thick white columns in front of it.

An arch driveway was in front, and so was a waterfall with black marble rock. I was so sure that they'd have an alarm system, but when I parked my car far down the street, and checked around the house, I didn't see one. I hoped like hell that no one was inside, and before entering the house, I waited around to be sure. The coast looked pretty clear to me, and when I tried the first key, it didn't work. The second key did, and the door opened up to a spacious, shiny hardwood foyer. Double staircases led to the upstairs and the big, arched picture windows in the back of the house allowed the sunset to show. The ceilings were high, and the house itself was unlike anything I had ever seen. In a magazine, maybe, but never, ever in real life. Everything was so tidy and clean, and before checking out the upstairs, I looked in the kitchen. The granite island took up most of the space, and it was surrounded with bar stools. Flat-screen TVs were throughout the house, and the backyard had a swimming pool with a Jacuzzi. Steven and Liz had it made, and as I saw the numerous pictures of them here and there, I had to admit that I was a little jealous. They made a great-looking couple, but, hopefully, that wouldn't be for long. I now wanted their marriage to end, only because a cheating man like Steven didn't deserve to live happily ever after.

I finally tackled the stairs, and my shoes sunk into the plush carpet. The master bedroom was the first thing that I saw, and it was to die for. A king-sized bed, dressed with black and gold silk sheets, sat against the wall. Two chaises were by the bay window, and a huge fireplace was in front of their bed. The bathroom made me want to get cozy, and I pictured myself in the oval-shaped, deep tub with Steven. I envisioned the candles being lit and him fucking my brains out. All I could do was regret that I hadn't demanded more of him. My rules were about to change, because I could definitely see myself someday living like this.

As I continued to look around upstairs, I heard the garage door open. My heart dropped to my stomach. I went back into the master bedroom, where I'd seen his-and-hers walk-in closets. Liz's closet was packed with clothes, shoes, hats, and purses, so I knew it would be easier for me to hide in there. I did, and wrapped myself with a comforter I'd seen in the far corner.

I could hear Liz on the phone talking to someone. I wasn't sure about moving just yet, so I stayed put.

"Me too," she said to the person on the phone. "I can't wait to get to church on Sunday to see how she reacts." She paused for a while. "I agree. I think she's screwing the pastor too, and the way he be looking at women drives me nuts. I'm going to find me another church to go to, soon." She laughed and paused again. "I know, and her dress! Did you see it last Sunday? That thing was up to her butt. She should know better, wearing something like that. I know you're supposed to come as you are, but that doesn't mean you should go to church looking like a tramp." She paused, then told the caller to hold on. "Yes, dear," she said. "Nothing, just talking on the phone to Cicely. She's running her mouth too much for me, so hold on a minute while I get her off this phone." She paused. "Cicely, this is my honey pooh. I'll talk to you later." There was silence for a minute. "Okay, babe, I'm back. Are we eating in or out tonight?" She listened to him speak. "Aw. Well, I'll throw something in the microwave for me, and you can pick up something on your way home. See you later and be careful." She paused before delivering the final blow. "I love you too, honey."

Fake, fake, fake was all I could think. I was somewhat worried about getting caught in the closet, and, more than anything, being arrested for breaking and entering. But seeing how these two operated at home was very interesting to me. Liz was just as I had expected, and, as I said, people really knew how to show their asses behind closed doors. The door to her closet opened, and I watched as she tossed a long silk robe over her shoulder. She removed her heels and placed them on a rack in front of her. She left the closet, closing the door behind her. I was actually in a pretty comfortable place in the closet, and as another hour and a half went by, I could hear the microwave going, and her yakking on the phone again. Then she came back into her room. I heard the bed squeak a little, then I heard the flat-screen TV that was above the fireplace come on. While on my knees, I crawled to the door, carefully turning the knob. I cracked the door a tiny bit, and saw Liz sitting on the bed, eating a Healthy Choice dinner. She was looking at the TV, and laughed at the reality show that she was watching.

"Terrible," she commented out loud. "These people should know better."

She finished her food, and left the plate on the tray.

I thought she was going to go back downstairs, but she didn't. She seemed tuned in to the TV, then picked up her cell phone again.

"Joy," she said. "Girl, are you watching *The Bachelor* tonight?" She paused. "I know. It's ridiculous, and he'd better not end up with that hoochie. I can't stand her, and if he picks her I am never watching this show again." She laughed, and when she heard the garage door go up, she told Joy she'd call her back. I saw her stretch and yawn while looking toward the doorway.

"Hello." She smiled as Steven walked into the room with a briefcase in his hand. He set it next to the bed and walked up to her. The same lips he used to suck my pussy were being placed on hers.

"Hey. How was your day?" he asked.

"Ugh," she said. "It was just okay. I tell you one thing, though. I am really getting sick of my job. Mr. Aimes is working me, and so are that darn Claudette and Chase. The way they look at each other drives me crazy. I've really got to do something to put my department at ease. It's not fun anymore. There was a time that we all used to have fun."

Steven was just nodding his head, I assumed, not paying her any attention, because he didn't respond. He sat on the edge of the bed, removing his shoes and wiggling his toes.

"I think my feet are growing, because my shoes are starting to get too tight."

"No, your feet aren't growing. Something else may be growing, but definitely not your feet."

Steven turned around to look at her, then snickered. He pulled off his jacket, then stood to go into his closet. He remained in there for a while, then walked back out in his boxers.

"What did you eat?" Liz asked.

"I had a sandwich. I really wasn't that hungry." He picked up his briefcase and set it on the bed. He removed some papers, then put the briefcase back on the floor. He joined Liz in bed, sitting up next to her. She was still tuned in to *The Bachelor,* and as she talked about the show, Steven stayed consumed with the papers in front of him. Liz got up to leave the room, and came back minutes later with two wineglasses. She gave one of them to Steven.

"Thank you," he said, pecking her lips again. "You're so sweet."

"I know. And so are you."

"Not as sweet as you are."

"As I said, I know."

They laughed, and as the night went on, they made small talk with each other. I was ready for the lights to go out, and for them to go to sleep, just so I could get the hell out of there. My back was starting to hurt and the closet was getting rather stuffy.

Liz kept flipping through the channels, and when she yawned, I felt relieved. She finally turned off the TV and scooted down in bed.

"I'm getting ready to go to sleep," she said, puckering her lips. Steven leaned over and kissed her.

"Good night. I'm going to shut it down in a minute too."

Liz turned her back, and Steven continued to sit up, observing the papers in front of him. He shook his head a few times, scratched his arm, then looked over at Liz. He stared at her for a few minutes, then laid the papers on his nightstand. He scooted down in bed, cradling the back of Liz.

"Baby," he whispered. "Have you gone to sleep yet?"

"Almost." She remained with her back facing him, and when his hands started to roam over her body, I was heated. He lifted her leg over his, and, from her moans, I could tell he was touching something. Maybe this wasn't such a good idea. It surprised me how peaceful things really appeared to be with them at home. It may have been a little boring, but, based on what my eyes saw next, maybe not.

Liz climbed on top of Steven and he lifted her long silk nightgown over her head, exposing her nakedness. He eased down his boxer shorts, kicking them to the edge of the bed. I watched as his boxers fell to the floor in front of my peeping eyes. Liz started to ride him and the look in his eyes displayed that he was very much into her.

"Ahh," he moaned. "I love you . . . love this. Do your thing, baby, and keep on giving it to me like this."

"I love you too," she said, riding him for a while longer, then turning herself around. Her face could be seen right through the crack of the closet, so I got a good look at her facial expressions. Steven had gotten behind her and was thrusting himself into her. Not quite as hard as he entered me, but more gentle. Her eyes were closed and she was licking around her top lip. "Ohh, Stevie," she whined. "Stevie, honey, this feels magnificent. Go in deeper. You know how much I like it when you go deep. Keep making me feel this good, every day, for the rest of my life!"

"Stevie" went in deeper, and Liz cut up just as much as me. She was panting like a dog, and he was grinding inside of her like there was no tomorrow. After all of the sex we'd been having, I was surprised that he still had so much energy. My insides were boiling. I wanted to pull the door open and tell him to go fuck himself, along with that trip he had mentioned to Vegas. I guess I shouldn't have been as upset as I was; after all, she was his wife. But seeing this shit for myself just did something to me. And just as I thought they were about to shut it down, he suggested that they go take a shower. I heard the water come on, and while in the closet, I could hear him pounding her against the wall. With each thud, she groaned out loud, telling him how much she loved him. He threw it back to her too, and as they continued, I rushed out of the closet to leave.

For the next several days, I answered not one of Steven's calls. He was like, "Where are you, sweetness? Why haven't I heard from you?" Had the nerve to even say he missed me, and when the Vegas weekend came, I was missing in action. I let my cell phone ring and ring, and refused to answer his calls. Just so I didn't have to stay cooped up in the house, I called Veronica to see if she wanted to go to the movies. That helped clear my head, and before the movie got started, we chomped on buttered popcorn. I started to tell her about what had happened at Liz's house that day.

"I was hiding in the closet, watching the action with a close-up view. My back was killing me, though, and when they went to the shower to finish up, I got the hell out of there."

Veronica's mouth was wide open. She kept shaking her head in disbelief. "You never cease to amaze me. Weren't you scared? I would have been shaking all over. What if they would have come in that closet and seen you?"

"If that would've happened, I would have busted out Steven. I was more concerned about being arrested for breaking and entering than I was about being caught by them. But what I saw really shocked me."

"Why? You had to know he was still having sex with his wife, didn't you?"

"Of course. But these men be acting like they're so unhappy at home with their wives, but many of them are not. They just enjoy having their cake and eating it too, and I don't like feeling as if I'm being used. I didn't expect him to be that aggressive with her, and, honestly, it shocked me."

"I'm just in awe about the whole thing. So, have you spoken to him since then?"

"He's called, but I haven't answered his calls. We were supposed to go to Vegas this weekend, but so much for that. I'm not going anywhere with him until I start getting some of the things I want. Girl, you should have seen that house. Liz got it made, and somebody got some straight-up money. I know it's him, and it's time for him to pay up."

"Have you fallen for him? You always said this was a 'D' thing, nothing more, nothing less. I know you ain't trying to have a for-real relationship with him, are you?"

"I'm just talking a bunch of mess right now because I'm mad, maybe a little jealous. But if I ever get with a man, he'd better be bringing it like Steven. As for him, what in the hell can I do with a married man, other than fuck him? I'm far from being a fool, and Steven knows that. If I say something to him about Liz, that'll make me look weak. He admires the confidence and nonchalant attitude that I have about his marriage. We are definitely going to keep doing our thing, and it will be a long time before either of us gets tired."

We both laughed and quieted ourselves when the movie got started.

After the movie wrapped up, I dropped Veronica off at home and headed to my apartment. I was inside for about ten minutes, then I heard a knock at the door. I wasn't expecting anyone, but when I asked who it was, the person cleared his throat.

"Steven," he said.

I was surprised that he had come to my apartment, and figured he must have gotten my address from the file that I'd left at his office. I hurried to check myself in the mirror, and straightened a few pillows on my couch. A glass was on my living room table, so I quickly ran and put it in the kitchen sink. I took a deep breath, then pulled on the door, inviting him into my cozy apartment, which was nicely decorated, but could in no way compare to his house.

"Have you been getting my calls?" he asked, standing by the door. He was casually dressed in jeans and a button-down tan shirt.

"Yes. But I've been dealing with something personal, so I stepped back for a minute."

He slightly cocked his head back. "Stepped back? But what about our trip? I paid for two tickets to Vegas and had to go alone. I didn't know what was up. I thought something had happened to you."

I sat on the couch, tucking my leg underneath me. "No, I'm okay. As I said, I just had some personal issues, and I didn't want to involve you."

He walked around the table and took a seat at the other end of the couch. "You want to talk about these personal issues or what?"

I let out a deep breath and turned toward him. "Are you still having sex with your wife?"

He didn't hesitate. "Barely. Why? What's it to you?"

"I just wanted to know, especially since we have as much sex as we do."

He shrugged. "So? And what does that mean? Am I supposed to completely cut off sex with my wife because we've been overly active?"

"No, not at all. And before you get all bent out of shape about it, I was just asking."

"Well, you shouldn't be asking at all because it's really none of your business. When we started this, I warned you about these kinds of conversations. I'm not having them with you, and if you're getting to a point where you can't handle this, let me know. I'll back up, and you won't have to stress yourself about doing it."

I loved aggressive men, but smart-mouth, arrogant men, especially the ones with wives, drove me nuts. "I guess you're right," I said, removing my leg from underneath me and standing up. "Besides, I don't like to feel stressed. When I get over this ill feeling I have inside, I'll call you. If it doesn't disappear, then I guess you won't hear from me anytime soon."

I went to the door, opening it wide so Steven could exit. He got off the couch. I could tell his insides were boiling, but he played it smooth. "Whatever, baby. It's whatever."

"See you later, *Stevie*. Have a good night."

He stopped before exiting. "Don't call me that," he said.

"Why not? That's what your wife calls you, isn't it?"

"Maybe so. But you're not her."

"Wouldn't want to be. Ever."

He walked out and I closed the door behind him. Steven made one big mistake tonight, and that was lying to me. It wasn't rare that he was having sex with Liz, and she even blurted it out that night. She specifically said, "Keep making me feel this good, every day, for the rest of my life."

Just with her saying that, I knew it was on. I was going to sit back for a while, because I had a feeling how this would play itself out. Steven would reach out to me before I ever reached out to him again. For months, I prepared myself for something like this to happen, and whenever he called me again, I didn't want to be shacked up in hotels with him. I didn't want to be in the back seat of a car, or screwed on the couch in his office. I wanted to be in the bedroom at his house, and in his shower, just like he was with Liz. No exceptions. Never as his wife, but as his plaything when his marriage fell apart. No doubt, it was bound to happen.

Chapter 10

The company picnic was today and Forest Park was packed with people that I worked with and their families. I invited Lance to go with me. He didn't mind, and since he was already pretty cool with Veronica too, we sat at a picnic table playing cards with two other ladies named Jazel and Gina. They worked in another department, but were known for gossiping. We couldn't even play cards without them talking about everybody's business around us. At the moment, they were discussing Claudette. She brought another man to the picnic with her, and the two of them seemed awfully chummy. I had warned her before about bringing her man around others, but luckily for her, he wasn't my type.

Liz was there with Steven, and her ol' prissy self sat far away from everyone, underneath a tree. She had a blanket on the ground, and Steven rested back on the blanket while reading a business book. When the barbecue cooks yelled for everyone to come and get it, folks gathered in line with paper plates in their hands. Before people ate, Mr. Aimes stood up, giving a speech about how much he appreciated the work his employees had been doing. He congratulated Liz on the increasing sales, and everyone clapped. I was fake as ever, and when I saw Steven look my way, I turned my head. I went to the food line with Lance and Veronica, and watched some of the kids jump up and down on a huge bouncing castle filled with balls.

It was pretty hot outside, so I was dressed in a yellow halter that tied with two strings in the back. My blue jean shorts were pretty short, but had a one-inch cuff at the bottom. I wore white Nike tennis shoes and left my sandals at home, only because I knew we'd be playing volleyball.

After we ate, a group of coworkers gathered to play volleyball. Lance wanted to go against me and Veronica, so he opted for the other team. More men were on that team anyway, and where we played, it was right in front of where Steven and Liz were chilling on the blanket. At first, Steven remained absorted in his book, but when Liz walked away, that's when he sat up. I was laughing out loud, letting him know that I definitely wasn't hurt because he hadn't called me in almost three weeks. I even bent over a few times, just so he could look at what I knew he was missing. When the ball was served over my head, I ran to get it. It rolled right by Steven, and he picked it up. He tossed it to me.

"Thanks." I smiled and turned back around to continue the game.

The women had lost two games, and, by this time, I was tired as ever.

"Sore loser," Lance teased, picking me up and throwing me over his shoulder. I laughed loudly.

"He's looking," Lance said underneath his breath. "And you know who I'm talking about."

"Put me down," I yelled out. A few seconds later he did, but kept his arm around my waist. I would have kissed him, but since kids were around, I backed up and smiled. Not once did I look Steven's way, but I figured he was still checking me out. A few minutes after that, I noticed him going to his car. He left, but Liz remained behind. She made her rounds talking to people, and finally came over to our table to talk to us.

"It is hot out here, isn't it?" she said.

"Very," I replied. Everyone else nodded. She continued to talk to us, and when my cell phone vibrated, I stepped away from the table to take the call.

"Yes," I said, already seeing Steven's number.

"Get in your car and drive down the street. Make a left, and at the first street, make a right. I'll be parked on the corner."

I didn't bother to tell anyone I was leaving. I walked to my car, and followed the directions that Steven had given to me. He was leaned against his black BMW, wearing his shades and looking dynamite as ever. His khaki shorts revealed the muscles in his toned calves, and the dark purple polo was perfect against his cocoa skin.

I parked in front of his car, then got out to talk.

"What's up?" I asked, standing in front of him, squinting my eyes from the bright sun.

"You miss me yet?"

"No, not really. I don't like your attitude, and the more I think about how you have everything you need, and I don't, it bothers me."

He sighed. "Everything like what? What is it that you want?"

"I want respect, and don't you ever compare me to your wife. If you think she is so much better than me, then don't run your ass to me again. In addition to respect, I want sex at least three times a week, no excuses. If you can do better than that, you won't hear me complaining. Pertaining to money, my pockets are getting tired of being empty. They shouldn't have to be, especially if I'm giving myself to a man like you. This has nothing to do with you being my sugar daddy; it's all about you giving a little to get a lot in return. Fair is fair, wouldn't you agree?"

Steven held out his hands. "The sex is no problem, and as far as Liz is concerned, I will keep her name out of my mouth. The money, I'm not sure what you want, and you need to be a bit more specific."

"I need some spending money, Steven. What can you do or give to a woman who gives you so much? I deserve something, don't I?"

Steven stood looking at me for a moment, then reached into his pocket to retrieve his wallet. "I want to see you tonight," he said, then gave me a credit card. "There's a hundred-thousand-dollar credit limit on that card, and all that I ask is that you not max it out."

That put a tiny smile on my face. It was good to know that we were progressing in a way that was beneficial to us both. I took the card, holding it in my hand. "Where would you like to meet tonight?"

"The usual."

"No, I'm not feeling that."

"Then where?"

"At your house. Let's meet at your house."

He removed his glasses. "What? You know we can't go to my house."

"Steven, you can do anything that you want to do. I'm sick of meeting you at hotels, and I don't want you to come to my place. I need a change of atmosphere. I'm getting bored with the regulars."

"Well, we can't meet at my house tonight."

"What about next week, or the week after? Liz is going out of town the week after next, isn't she?"

"Yes, but I'm supposed to go with her."

"Then don't go."

He shrugged. "Maybe. But what about tonight?"

"I can't do tonight. The earliest I can do is Monday morning. I'll call in sick, and while Liz is at work, I can come to your house. What about that?"

Steven hesitated and sucked his teeth. "I feel what you're doing. You know you're putting me on the spot. If I say no, sex between us ain't happening any time soon, is it?"

"I'm afraid not. I told you a long time ago that I was a risk taker, and I'm in one of those places where I feel as if I need to start taking a bigger risk. You've struck me as being a big risk taker too. Starting your business from scratch, I'm sure you took plenty of risk. I really don't see what the big deal is."

"I'm a risk taker, but that's a big . . . huge risk. I'll let you know what I decide tomorrow night."

"Make sure you let me know ahead of time. Since we haven't been together in weeks, I promise to make it worth it."

"I'm sure you will," he said, watching me as I walked back to my car. I sped off, and since Veronica had driven to the park, I sent her a text, telling her something came up. I asked if she would take Lance home. Truth was, I had some major shopping to do, and couldn't wait to get myself a new bedroom set.

When Sunday night came, I waited for my call from Steven and got it. I couldn't believe the power of pussy, but, then again, yes, I could. Steven told me to come to his house at nine o'clock in the morning and he gave me directions. I assured him that I would be there, and left a message on Liz's phone to tell her I wasn't going to make it in tomorrow.

Morning was here before I knew it. I really hadn't gotten much sleep, thinking about my adventurous day. By 8:55 A.M., I was parked down the street from his house and had knocked on his door. Steven was in his robe, smelling good as ever. He had the phone pressed up to his ear, but grabbed my waist and pulled me inside. We stood in the foyer, and as he kept saying, "Uh-huh, yes," to the person on the other end, he playfully pecked down my neck. He squeezed my waist, pulling me into him and smiling his butt off. I was all smiles too, and as the person on the phone went on and on, I inched him back to the plush steps. I untied his robe, and he lay back on his elbows. Lowering myself, I gave him pleasure and sucked his goods while he remained on the phone. He could barely utter a word, and after rushing to tell the person he'd call them right back, he let the phone fall from his hands. It tumbled down the steps, landing in the foyer. I quickly brought Steven to an eruption, then crawled up a few more steps to straddle his face. I wore a very short skirt, but had on no panties. My wet slit touched his lips and when his tongue dipped into me, I was trembling all over. His performance was so good, and he held on to my thighs to keep me in place.

"I told you you'd enjoy this, didn't I?" I said. "I sure in the hell am, and I can't wait to get to your bedroom."

Steven worked me, and the oral sex exchange on the steps was just the beginning. We traveled from there to his bedroom, and then to the shower. We took a break around noon to get something to eat, and then ended our last session in his office in the basement. I was 110 percent satisfied, and as four o'clock rolled around, I finally put on my clothes to go.

"Are you happy now?" he said, standing by the front door with his hand on the knob.

"Maybe. Today, you showed me that you got game and guts. I like that."

"Not as much game as you, but I'm a big boy, and trust me, I can handle it."

I had no doubt that Steven could. I kissed him one last time before leaving, and he smacked my ass on the way out.

Things were back to normal, at least pertaining to Steven and me. I was glad to be back on track with him, but I was so disappointed with what had been going on at work. Liz had rescheduled her trip, pushing it back an additional three weeks. That was fine with me, but that meant I wouldn't be able to spend any time with Steven in their house. Liz was acting so cold toward everyone in the office, and since her coldness was not just directed at me, I didn't take it personally.

Mr. Aimes had come in a few times to talk to her, and whenever he left, she was in a tizzy. I figured he was on her again about sales, but maybe she should have been a bit more focused on her job. Liz had gone off on Claudette so badly the other day, she sent Claudette's ol' sensitive self to the bathroom in tears. Liz's type of going off was just her raising her voice, or her correcting you when you were wrong. Claudette had lied about mailing some invoices, and the customers didn't get them on time. Liz looked through her desk after work one day, and found the invoices tucked at the side of Claudette's computer. She looked so stupid when Liz told her she'd found them, and all that idiot could do was cry. Whenever Liz got after me like that, I challenged her back. I rarely made mistakes, but lately my mind was a bit preoccupied. I was making more mistakes than usual, and you'd better believe that Liz caught every little thing. She brought it to my attention, and sighed when I came up with an excuse about why it happened.

"I probably got interrupted by my phone, but I am human and I will make some mistakes."

"Don't let it happen again," she spat, then went into her office and closed the door.

I reminded myself to ask Steven if he knew what was up with her, and when I finally told him about her attitude at work, he simply said that she was frustrated with her job.

"She's had a lot going on, Chase, so don't take her actions personally. She is perfectly fine at home, and if anything changes, I'll be sure to give you a heads-up."

I thanked Steven and ended the call. I figured Liz hadn't known anything either, as she had proven herself to be the kind of person who would quickly call you on your shit. I wasn't too worried about that, but I was concerned about my job. Steven had set up an interview for me with a friend at his office, working as his secretary. He wanted me to get away from Liz as quickly as possible, and said that it would put less strain on what was going on behind closed doors. He could tell that I was bitter when it came to her. Even though I used to like Liz a lot, I had changed my mind. Not only because of her husband, but because she was really fake. She had been smiling in our faces for months, but deep down, she couldn't stand any of us. I thought Claudette was her favorite, but as it turned out, the only person Liz was okay with was Veronica. Why? Because she stayed out of Liz's way, and the one thing I liked about Veronica was, she never, ever tried to kiss Liz's ass. I liked how Veronica backed off when Liz tried to jump into her personal business about Tony, and ever since then, Liz hadn't said one word to Veronica about that night at the Christmas party.

We were busy as ever, and as I was trying to do my work, I heard Claudette whispering on the phone to someone. I figured it was that nappy-head fool she had brought to the picnic with her, and when I heard her say his name, it confirmed I was right. She was giggling a lot, and the last time I checked, Liz had deadlines for all of us. I hadn't heard Claudette's fingers typing on those invoices all day, but Veronica was behind me doing her thing. Now, she may have been a snacker, and I would hear bags of chips and other snacks crackling all day. She was always tossing something over my cubicle for me to eat, and she was known for downing a lot of sodas. That's where most of her weight came from, and since I'd been hanging with Veronica, I had picked up a pound . . . maybe two. I at least had her working out with me on some mornings, and, before coming to work, I'd tell her to meet me at the gym. She met me one or two days a week, but everybody had to start somewhere.

As I continued to type Liz's letter, Claudette's giggling and whispers were becoming annoying. Veronica had already emailed me, asking if Claudette was up there doing any work. I responded, *"Hell no,"* and Veronica was livid. Since she and Claudette did the same kind of work, the burden would fall on her. Veronica got out of her seat, and stood in front of Claudette's cubicle.

"Excuse me," Veronica said, interrupting Claudette's phone call. "Uh, we have less than three hours to get this work done. Those papers on my desk have not moved, and I'm not going to sit here and do all of this by myself, especially while you're up here on the phone. You've been on it for at least an hour. I wish you would save the conversation with your man for later."

"Hold on, snookums," Claudette said into the phone. Without even looking over my cubicle, I knew her neck was rolling off her shoulders. "Excuse me, but I have only been on the phone for ten minutes. Don't be coming over here trying to tell me what to do. I'll get those papers off your desk as soon as I get off the phone."

"You have not been on the phone for ten minutes. There are people around here who will vouch for me, especially if I have to go tell Liz about this. If she asks why those invoices aren't done, you'd better believe that when she comes out of her office, I plan to tell her."

Claudette finally told trick daddy to call her back. She stood up to confront Veronica. I had to give it to the chick, she really had guts. Veronica was a pretty big girl, and one blow from her would send Claudette flying backward. "I don't give a care who you get to vouch for you. I assume it will be your playmate, Chase, and who gives a darn what she thinks? She'll side with you anyway, and if you want to go tell Liz on me like a little whiny child, then go ahead and do it. I'm shaking in my seat. I'm so, so scared."

I was doing my best not to intervene, but why did my name have to come out of her mouth? She knew we weren't on good terms already, and if she wanted to play the bully, then she deserved to get confronted. I stood, looking into her cubicle. "Please keep my name out of your mouth. This issue is between you and Veronica. I have nothing to do with it."

She rolled her eyes and threw her hand back at me. "Shut up and sit down. I'll say what I want to, slut, and you're not going to do a darn thing about it."

"No, I'm not. Only because you're not worth my time, Claudette. You're still bitter because I had sweat-dripping sex with your man, and you really need to get over it."

I sat in my chair, but she kept at it. She looked over at me this time, as her situation with Veronica was no longer an issue. "That's what trashy women do, Chase. They sleep with other people's men, because they can't find one of their own. Too bad Korey fell for it, but he's a whore just like you, so it really doesn't matter."

"Don't cry about it," I said, noticing her get all worked up. I was so done with Korey, but I wanted to infuriate her even more. "And when you get done calling me names and suggesting that I'm such a whore, you know what, you're right. That's why I'm still having sex with Korey, and that freaky stuff you wouldn't allow him to do, he does with me. He asked how you were doing the other day, and I told him you were still the ol', big-lip, bitter bitch he left standing at the fantasy wedding looking stupid."

Her face was turning red and her voice was getting louder. "Oh, you don't—"

Liz's door flew open, and she stood with her hand on her hip. "Please do not tell me that the two of you are at it again. Into my office," she ordered. "Now!"

Claudette walked with a mean mug on her face, but I was calm as ever. Veronica looked a bit upset too, and she came in behind me, just so she could tell Liz how all of this got started. I hated to act like a kindergartner, but Claudette made me go there. She and I took a seat, but Veronica stood by the door.

Liz took off her glasses and laid them on her desk. "I can't believe the two of you are still going at it over a man. What is up with this? Is he worth the two of you losing your jobs?"

Before I could tell Miss Liz that she was wrong again, Veronica chimed in and told her what had happened. Claudette defended herself, but Liz stopped her. She pointed to the green lights on her phone.

"You see these buttons right here?" she said. "When they are lit up, I can see exactly who is on the phone and for how long. Claudette, your phone has been lit up three or four times today, for too, too long. I told all of you that I needed to get these invoices out of here, and my letters needed to be typed and mailed today. The files in my office are backing up, and all you ladies can do is sit out there and argue with each other. Are we back in kindergarten or something? I thought you all were grown women. I can't tell you all how disappointed I am."

"I apologize, Liz," I said. "And I've done my best to stay out of Claudette's way. There is only so much a person can take, and I can't accept being at work and being called bitch and ho. I have never attacked Claudette in such a way, and she knows it. I have always tried to conduct myself with professionalism in here, but it is difficult working with someone like Claudette who doesn't have the same work ethic."

Claudette's mouth was open. I reached over and lifted her chin to close it. She smacked my hand, calling me a stupid bitch. Plan B went into action. What do you do to a woman who continues to disrespect you at work? You slap the shit out of her. That's what I did, and it was something I had wanted to do for a long, long time. Liz jumped up from her seat, but before she made it around her desk to get between us, Claudette pushed my chest.

"Don't put your hands on me, heifer," she yelled.

"Stop it!" Liz hollered, standing between us. Veronica had one of my arms, but I was in no way going to hit Claudette again. I got the smack that I wanted, and quite frankly, I enjoyed seeing my handprint on her face.

"Pack your things," Liz ordered. "And both of you get out. You're fired! I'm not going to do this. I will get some of the other women from the other departments to assist me."

I had already figured that something like this would happen, so I wasn't going to sit there and defend my situation to Liz. I left her office, and started gathering my things to go. Veronica offered to help, but I declined her offer. I told her we would talk later, and thirty minutes later, I was out the door. Claudette had left before I did and that was a good thing.

On my drive home, my cell phone started to ring. I looked to see who it was. It was Steven.

"Hello," I said sharply.

"Please tell me that what Liz just called and told me was a lie. I know you didn't go out like that at work, did you?"

"I'm not sure what Liz told you, and I'm sure she made me look like a villain. Claudette went too far today, and I basically let her have it."

"As calm and collected as you are when we're together, I can't even see you doing anything like that. The interview is still set up for you with my friend, but I can't guarantee that you'll get the job."

"I'll give it my all in the interview. Hopefully, your friend will feel I'm qualified and hire me. If not, I'll look somewhere else. I'm not going to stress myself out about it. As you said before, this may all turn out for the best anyway."

"I agree, but I don't like that you got fired. I'll check back with you later, and if that particular opportunity doesn't work out, I have a few other connections. I'll see what else I can do."

I hung up. It was good to know that Steven had my back. It wasn't like I could take weeks and weeks off

without pay, but I at least had his credit card to help
with my wants and needs.

  The following week, I was hired to work as a secretary for Steven's friend, Josh. He was an older white
guy, and he seemed pretty pleasant. The office envi-
ronment was quite different than the one I was used
to, and there were definitely less people. Probably a
total of ten people in the whole building, but that was
fine by me. My salary increased by $500, and even
though it wasn't much, I was pleased that I didn't have
to take a pay cut. I only had to work from Monday
through Thursday, too, giving me a three-day weekend
that I promised myself I would enjoy.
  Steven liked my hours too, and with Fridays off,
that gave us time to hook up in the morning. I was
starting to get comfortable at his house, and we were
always so very careful. He kept in contact with Liz
throughout the day, making sure that she was at work,
where she was supposed to be. And while she was, I
was at her house preparing lunch for her husband and
screwing his brains out. I was surprised that I hadn't
gotten sick of Steven yet, nor did he seem to be tired of
me.
  When the weekend arrived, I knew I'd be lonely because Steven said that he would be away on business,
and we wouldn't be able to hook up until the following
week. Liz was still scheduled to go out of town in a few
weeks, but her trip wasn't coming soon enough for
me. Instead of doing nothing, I went over to Lance's
apartment to see if he wanted to go out and do something. He insisted that he wasn't feeling well. He let me

come into his apartment, but he went back to the couch to cuddle with a body pillow.

"Do you want me to make you some chicken noodle soup?" I said, teasing him.

He pulled the blanket over his head and coughed. "No. And you'd better get out of here before you get sick. If you happen to leave, though, please bring me some orange juice. I don't have nothing to drink, and my throat is a little dry."

"I have some at my apartment. I'll go get it for you."

Lance coughed again and I went over to my apartment to get the orange juice. The container was pretty full, so I poured a tall glass for me, and left it in my refrigerator. I carried the carton across the hall to him, but I noticed that his door was open. I knew I had closed it, but as soon as I heard a woman's voice coming from his apartment, I went inside.

"Why do you lie so much, Lance?" The woman took off her shoe and threw it at him. "I am so done with you. Do not call me anymore."

Lance was sitting up on the couch, and he tossed her shoe back at her. "Okay, whatever. I promise that I won't call you anymore, so leave, please."

The woman looked at me. "Who are you? If you're another one of his girlfriends, or if you're considering becoming one, please don't waste your time. He's a scumbag."

She didn't have to tell me. I already knew that, and that was the main reason why I had not pursued a relationship with him. I held up the carton of orange juice. "I'm just his neighbor. He asked me for some orange juice and I'm bringing it to him."

She looked me up and down, then took off her other

shoe and threw that one at Lance too. He ducked, ordering her to leave before he called the police. She called him a jerk, and left his apartment without her shoes. Now, I wouldn't have ever left my shoes. She was tripping. I closed Lance's door and locked it.

"Wow," I said. "So, you got a psycho woman on your hands, huh?"

"You know how y'all women do it. I've told her time and time again that it ain't that serious, but she ain't trying to hear it."

"And I'd bet you any amount of money that you weren't saying that when you were in between her legs."

Lance chuckled, seriously thinking the shit was funny. Some men just had no shame in their game, and nice guy or not, there wasn't a chance in hell that I would ever date Lance. Men of his caliber came in all different shapes, forms, and fashions. They didn't have to be the finest thing you'd ever seen, nor the wealthiest. It was just the thing to do, and nine times out of ten, a woman could easily find herself caught up.

"Listen," Lance said. "Let's go somewhere and get something to eat. I'm hungry as hell, and there ain't no need for me to be sitting up in here, making myself feel more miserable by lying on this couch."

"Let's go," I said. "But I'm driving. You look like you're about to pass out. Maybe some fresh air is what you need."

Lance and I went to Houlihan's in the West End. The restaurant was very cozy and had a dim setting. Lit candles were placed on the tables, and they were covered with crisp white tablecloths. Several ceiling fans hung over our heads, giving me a slight chill that

I in no way minded, only because I was in the mood for my favorite stuffed mushrooms and couldn't wait to dive into them. We were seated by a huge glass picture window and could see outside to the hundreds of people walking down the busy streets. Many cars drove by; mainly expensive ones, as we were in an upscale neighborhood.

"All I want is some baked chicken," Lance said, rubbing his forehead.

"Do you want some aspirin? You should have taken some before you left."

"If you have some in your purse, please hand them over."

I dug into my purse, then gave Lance two aspirin. He popped them in his mouth, then sipped from the glass of water on the table. After the waiter took our orders, Lance seemed to perk up.

"So, are you liking your new job?" he asked.

"It's okay. It may take some time for me to get used to."

"That was nice of your sugar daddy to look out for you. I guess that's what they do."

"Steven is not my sugar daddy. He is a good friend who I enjoy being with."

"I hear you. But didn't you tell me that he paid your rent and car payment this month?"

"Yes."

"Then he's your sugar daddy."

"No, he is not. If that's the case, then you got plenty of sugar mamas. How many times have you told me someone gave you something, and didn't you show me a card and teddy bear one of your women gave you for Valentine's Day?"

Lance laughed. "That is not the same thing and you know it. And you are only assuming that I got all of these women. I may have a few, but nowhere near what you think."

"Lance, please. Last week alone, I think I bumped into at least three or four different women, coming and leaving your apartment."

"And?"

"And that's pretty pathetic. How many women do you need?"

"I only need one, but I haven't found the right one yet. As for the women you see, you should never be on the outside looking in. Your eyes may deceive you."

"And how is that? I know what I see going on, and you, my dear, are definitely a player."

"I couldn't handle all of those women if I tried. As a matter of fact, I am dating two women who I thought were satisfied with the open relationship we have. The woman you saw tonight was one of those women, but she's canceled for throwing her shoes at me."

"Then, what about all of those other women?"

"Those women are my clients."

My brows went up in curiosity. "Clients? Are you a pimp or something?"

Lance laughed. "No. I'm a private counselor, who is paid by the state. I counsel women about their relationships, and try to help them make better lives for themselves and their families. I've been doing it for the past five years. I didn't want to tell you because I didn't want you to think that's why I was befriending you. Yes, I think you have some issues, but you mentioned that you'd been in counseling. I hope it's helping."

I was shocked, but wasn't sure if I could believe

DON'T EVEN GO THERE   173

Lance. "Don't play with me," I said. "Why haven't you said this to me before?"

"I just told you, and I couldn't think of a better time. Besides, my job is very confidential. When you're accusing me of being a pimp and calling me a playboy, that really isn't the case."

"But you do have more than one woman, don't you?"

He defensively held his hands in the air. "Well, I'll be damned. Shoot me. Most single men do have more than one woman, and that's why they call themselves single. Some married men have more than one woman, but we definitely don't want to go there. You, of all people, know how that is."

"I sure do, and that's why I don't trust men. Y'all are some devious and conniving creatures. I don't believe that there are any faithful men left on this planet."

"We're out there, but women like you aren't interested in finding us. You already have your mind made up that faithful men don't exist, so a search for one, in your book, is useless. The first day you meet a guy, you're already telling yourself that he ain't shit and he's going to wind up breaking your heart and he's just like all the others. But he very well may not be.

"You gotta give some of these brothers a chance to show you what they're working with, and if you're not feeling him, then step. You'll never find the kind of man you need in your life, especially if you continue to waste your time on a married man. Time is just passing you by, Chase, and I'm serious when I say to you that one day you're going to regret not seeing things for what they truly could be."

"Maybe that day will come, or maybe not. Believe it

or not, I'm content with the way things are in my life. For now, I wouldn't have it any other way."

Lance and I continued our discussion, and after the advice he'd given me, I wholeheartedly believed he was a counselor. A lot of what he'd said made sense, but he just didn't realize that everybody's situation was different. Some women had never been burned by a man, then there were others who kept getting burned over and over. At some point, when Plan A didn't work, you always had to consider Plan B. My Plan B was to set love aside for a while and use men for the only thing I needed from them. That, of course, was sex.

The waiter brought our food to the table. Lance's baked chicken looked so good that I reached my fork across the table and poked into his chicken to get a piece. I put it into my mouth, and closed my eyes because it tasted so good. "Mmmm," I said, opening my eyes to tell him how good the chicken was. Instead, my eyes were glued to the black BMW that I saw pass by the window. I swore it was Steven's car, but even from a distance, I could tell the woman on the passenger's side was not Liz. Besides, I knew Steven's vehicle like I knew the back of my hand, and I was positive that was it. I quickly wiped my mouth with a napkin.

"I'll be right back," I said to Lance.

"Where are you going?"

I couldn't even answer, as I was moving so quickly to see what was up. Traffic was moving at a slow pace, and when I got outside, I saw the BMW pull over to the curb. When the door opened on the passenger's side, I saw her silver, strapped, high-heeled shoes and darker-skinned legs step out of the car. When she came out, she looked about my age, but was much thicker than I was. Steven got out looking spectacular as ever, suited up in a dark green suit. I stayed far enough back where he couldn't see me, and as I watched them cut across the street to go to an exquisite restaurant, I wasn't quite sure about their connection. It was revealed to me when I noticed him take her hand and escort her to a table. He pulled the chair back for her, and after she took a seat, he took one too. I could see them chatting through the tall glass windows, and I wasn't quite sure how to handle this. By all means, he wasn't my man, and we did have an understanding. Thing was, though, he'd lied to me about being out of town. Why lie? That's what I didn't understand. It made me feel as if I were being made a fool of, and made him look like he was full of shit. I wasn't even bothered by the fact that I was his homegirl, and that he had never taken me to dinner. If I wanted dinner, I could have gotten it at any given time. Just like the credit card he had given me. If I wanted more, I could have gotten it. All I asked was for Steven to not lie to me about his personal relationships, and there he was, lying his ass off about being out of town. I wasn't his wife, but an explanation was needed.

I wasn't dressed to impress, but the white linen sundress I wore did look decent. I had on silver flat sandals, and I at least had sense enough to brush up my makeup before I'd left. I entered the restaurant, telling the waiter that my guests were already waiting for me. Steven and the woman sat at a square table, with four chairs around it. The table was covered with a crisp white tablecloth, and had a candle in the middle of it. His pearly whites were in full effect, as the woman was saying something to him. I couldn't hear what it was, but when I got closer, he was just beginning to speak. I interrupted.

"I thought that was you," I said, standing next to him. "I thought you were going out of town this weekend."

Just by the look in his eyes, I knew that this woman was not a friend. He sat up straight, softly rubbing the trimmed hair on his chin. "I had a change of plans, so I didn't go. I will, however, give you a ring later."

Now, he didn't think I would just walk away and say okay, did he? I reached out my hand to the woman and introduced myself.

"Hi. My name is Chase Jenkins. I'm mistress number one, and who are you? Mistress number two?" I looked at Steven, pointing to myself. "Am I one or two, I can't remember."

He just sat there, looking at me like I was crazy.

"Come on now, Steven, quit playing. I figured that since you were screwing me at least three or four times a week, I'd be considered your number one. But by the look on her face, I'm not really sure. Help a sista out and please clarify some things for me. Please."

He sucked his teeth and his cold eyes looked like they were shooting daggers at me. "You want clarification. I'll give you clarification. Chase, meet my daughter, Britney. Britney, this is a woman who has lost her motherfucking mind." He stood up, and all I could think was, *Oh, shit!* I had really messed up, and my heart had already dropped to my stomach. My face was cracked all over the floor, but it was too late to try to pick it up. Steven excused himself from his daughter, telling her that he'd be right back. I really didn't want to follow him, but what else was I supposed to do? Plan B wasn't coming quick enough for me, and I wished it would hurry up.

Steven stepped outside of the restaurant, waiting for me to come down the steps.

"You fucked up," he said with his hands in his pockets. "Damn, you fucked up."

I quickly tried reverse psychology. "No, you fucked up. You told me that you were going out of town. What was I supposed to think? Besides, you and Liz don't even have any children. Since when did you have a daughter?"

"Not that it's any of your business, but I had her before I met Liz. I can't believe you just did what you did, and you'd better hope like hell that I can clear this mess up."

"And if not, is it going to be the end of the world for me? I don't think so. Now, I apologize for what just happened, but don't—"

Steven started to walk away from me. "Damn you, Chase. And to hell with your apology."

He jogged up the steps and went back into the restaurant. I stood for a moment, thinking that maybe, just maybe, I'd overreacted. Thinking about what I'd done, I quickly made my way back to the restaurant where Lance was. I plopped down in the chair, and looked at the almost empty plate in front of me. Lance was forking up the last of my mushrooms.

"You did not lie. Those stuffed mushrooms were too good. I didn't know if you were coming back, and the way you broke out of here, I suspected not. I'm sure you're going to tell me what happened, and by the look on your face, I can tell it wasn't good."

"Let's just say that you were right about some things you said tonight and I was wrong. It's wrong to assume anything, and doing so will mess you up every time."

"I'm glad you recognize that. Now, tell me what happened."

I told Lance what happened, and he was shaking his head with every word that left my mouth. I asked him to comment, but he wouldn't. We left the restaurant arm in arm. I laid my head on his shoulder, and Lance jokingly patted the side of my head.

"You'll be okay, baby, trust me."

Normally, I wouldn't even trip, but I never liked making a complete fool of myself. This time, I'd gone overboard, and it wasn't like me to trip off any man who was willing to play by my rules like Steven had.

Chapter 11

Okay. There is a time in a woman's life when she has to realize that she may have been wrong about some things. During my time, unfortunately, I had to stoop to an all-time low and kiss a little ass. I didn't want to, but since this was such a rare occasion, why not? Steven hadn't called me all week, and as I spoke to his voice mail, I tried to sound as pathetic, and as convincing as I could.

"I so apologize for the other night. I truly don't know what got into me. I hope you were able to work everything out with your daughter, and if you were, I'd love to hear from you. Call me."

There, I did it. I apologized, again, and if that wasn't good enough, I figured I could always try something else.

At the end of the week, I still hadn't heard from Steven. And you know what I said before about kissing a little ass? No, scratch that shit. No man's ass was worth kissing, and if he couldn't accept my apology, to hell with him. He was the one who said he could handle this, and, being a risk taker, didn't he prepare himself for something like this happening? Well, he should have, and if he didn't, that was a dumb move on his part.

I needed a break from all that had been going on, and when all else had failed, my Plan B was to take a trip, paying for it with the credit card that was burning hot in my pocket. Veronica and I had talked about taking a vacation, and since I didn't have to work on Fridays, she and I cut out early Friday morning to go on our cruise. By two o'clock, our plane had arrived at the airport in Miami, and a taxi driver took us to the port. Cruise ships were lined up for days, and since Veronica had never been on a cruise, she was overly excited.

"Girl, I can't believe I'm about to get on one of those big cruise boats. They are huge! I had no idea they were that big."

Veronica followed me, and we waited in a long line as our passports were checked by customs, and our baggage was scanned. Afterward, we were given numbers, and when our numbers were called, we were allowed to take pictures before entering the ship. As we stepped on, Veronica's eyes were bugged as ever. She couldn't believe how many levels the cruise boat had, but I was sure she would enjoy the best thing about it, and that was the food. The moment we checked into our cabins, we changed into our swimming gear and hurried to the upper level to get our grub on. My two-piece hot pink bikini was working magic, but I couldn't say much for Veronica. The black one-piece swimming suit that she wore was too plain. She covered herself with a sheer wrap, so it didn't look too bad. She felt a bit insecure, but I reminded her that we were there to have fun. She needed this break and so did I.

We hurried to the upper level of the ship, where there was so much food. You best believe that Veronica's plate was piled high with chicken, fruits, desserts, and she even threw in a salad. My plate was stacked too, but since there was a workout room on the boat, I told Veronica that would be the first place we would go in the morning. She agreed.

As we sat getting our grub on, my eyes scanned the hundreds and hundreds of people around us. In particular, the men. I had to see what they were working with, and I had already seen a few men I intended to get to know before the weekend was over. One so-so man was waving at me from afar, and all I did was smile at him. I got back to the food in front of me, and since Veronica hadn't even taken a second to breathe, she definitely didn't have time to talk.

"Girl, that food ain't going nowhere. We have all weekend, and wait until you see the array of food they are going to bring out."

"If it gets any better than this," she said, "I'm in trouble."

"Me too," I laughed.

For the next few hours, Veronica and I walked around the ship, looking at everything in sight. There was so much to do, and we talked about returning to some of the clubs that night, going to the karaoke bar, gambling, watching the dancers on stage . . . and, of course, more eating. We stopped at some of the shops to buy some souvenirs, and we had taken so many pictures so we could see them displayed on the ship later.

Veronica started to complain about her feet hurting, and since her ankles had swelled, she wanted to go back to the cabin to relax. I wasn't ready to go back to the cabin just yet, so I told her I'd catch up with her later. She left, and I continued to browse the ship. I bought another camera because I'd left mine on the plane, and I also bought a straw hat so I wouldn't burn myself when I sat out in the sun. I was ready to relax, so I went to the upper level and found an empty lounging chair. I lay back in the chair, and after I put on some sunscreen, I let the sun bake my body. The feel of being on the ocean, with the ship coasting through the water, was the best feeling ever. I had cleared my head and drowned out all of the noise around me. My eyes were closed, but no one could see them behind the dark shades I wore. I could almost feel myself going to sleep, but as soon as I heard that first snore, I felt someone touch my leg.

"Excuse me," he said.

My eyes popped open, seeing a young black man with red swimming trunks in my view. He looked okay, but I was irritated that he interrupted me. "Yes."

"Sorry to bother you, but my name is Kurt. Are you here with someone?"

"Yes."

"Male or female."

I lied, just to get him to back off. "Female, but for the record, I'm not interested in men."

He stepped back. "Oh, sorry about that, but I sure wish that you were."

"No, sorry."

He shook my hand and walked away. I hated to go there, but if I didn't, I sensed he would be on my back for the remainder of the cruise. I definitely didn't want that because he was in no way my type.

I turned onto my stomach, resting my head on my arms. I started to fade off again, but this time, not for long. I knew that we had a late dinner scheduled for 8:00 P.M., so after I lay for a while longer, I left to go to my cabin. Before going to my room, I stopped at Veronica's room to check on her. I couldn't believe she had been asleep, and she yawned when she opened the door.

"Are you that bored?" I asked. "There is all kinds of stuff to do on this ship, and you got the nerve to be in there sleeping."

"It's been a long, long day. The airplane ride was long, then we had to get on this ship and do all of that walking. That food did it for me, so I had to shut it down. I'm rested now, and as soon as I change clothes, we can go and do whatever."

Veronica asked me what she should put on, and I advised her to keep it simple. We had to dress up for Saturday's dinner, but tonight was casual night. She showed me a simple khaki top and capris that she'd gotten from Ashley Stewart, so I told her to put that on. I went to my cabin and put on a plain mustard fitted sundress that had a pink sunflower near my shoulder. My pink and mustard sandals matched perfectly, and I prepared myself for a lengthy night ahead of me.

Needless to say, we had a blast that night. After dinner, we stopped in at some of the clubs, dancing our hearts out. One thing I liked about cruises is everybody was there to have fun. There were so many intoxicated people, and it was hilarious to watch them make fools of themselves. I had a bit much to drink too, but I knew how to contain myself. So did Veronica, and as we went from one club to the next, we stayed on the dance floor. All kinds of men were dancing with us, and even ladies too. Veronica took her chances with karaoke, and I was surprised by how well she did. Whistles and applause were given by the crowd, but, unfortunately, she didn't win the big prize. I hadn't had this much fun in a long time, and I promised myself that I wouldn't think about anything or anyone back at home. My cell phone was tucked away somewhere in my cabin, and I couldn't even remember where I had put it.

Around two o'clock in the morning, we decided to call it a night. The ship was expected to arrive in the Bahamas at 8:00 A.M., and I had to get some kind of rest before then. As we made our way to our rooms, Veronica was acting silly. She was singing loudly and speaking to everybody who passed by us. The people were very friendly, and one fool had the nerve to place his face next to hers, singing with her. I was too embarrassed, and as I walked off laughing, I was stopped in my tracks. In front of me was a super gorgeous white man. He reminded me of David Beckham, and his cut frame could be seen from a distance. The black pants he wore fit his waist perfectly, and from the way he swaggered toward me, I knew I had to have it. Veronica rushed up to me.

"Do you see what I see?" she said underneath her breath.

"Don't you notice the direction of my eyes?"

He got closer to us, but only smiled as he walked by. Veronica and I both were caught in a trance by his olive green eyes, and I put my fist in my mouth to prevent myself from screaming. He should have been in a magazine, or, if not, definitely on somebody's runway.

Veronica rubbed my back. "Calm down," she said. "I know. We'll look for him tomorrow, and if you do not get him to come to your cabin, I swear to you that I will get him to come to mine!"

I laughed. "But . . . but what if he's here with someone? A man that fine didn't come here alone."

"Since when did that stop you? Who cares if he's with somebody? Besides, we're fine too, and look at us. We didn't come with anybody."

I nodded. "You may have a point. I'll definitely have to check on him tomorrow."

I could feel the cruise ship rock back and forth, but was too darn tired to get seasick. Morning came too fast, and the captain's announcement and that darn bell chiming woke me up. I pulled the curtain aside and could see that the ship was docked. I showered and changed into my bikini, but wore blue jean shorts to cover my bottom half. I left my room to go to Veronica's, but when I got there she didn't open the door. I was a bit worried, but when I went to the upper level, I saw her sitting close to the edge, eating breakfast with a man. She waved for me to come sit down.

"Hey, girl," she said. "This is A.J. He wanted to join me for breakfast, that's if you don't mind."

A.J. spoke to me, and I spoke back. I looked at Veronica. "You could have at least woken me up and told me you were coming up here to eat breakfast."

"I knew you hadn't gotten much sleep, so I didn't want to wake you. Besides, I couldn't sleep last night with all of that rocking going on, so I stayed up last night. I met A.J. while I was on my way up here."

I shook my head and went inside to get something to eat. Yes, I told myself that I was going to work out, but who wanted to be on a treadmill when the view out here was so beautiful? The bluish green water and sandy beaches were in view, and so were the blowing palm trees. Many other ships were lined up next to us, and yachts were in the water as well. Since I didn't work out, I was cautious about what I ate. My body looked too good to mess up, and with all of the attention it got me, I in no way wanted to go overboard with the food. I had seen the men's heads turning and the finger pointing going on. I wasn't interested in anyone but the man from last night, who had made me see fireworks. If he was on the cruise with someone else, too bad. I'd have to somehow work around her.

When I spotted him eating at one of the tables with a woman in an itty-bitty bikini, I kept my eyes on the prize. They were sitting next to the fruit bar, so I made my way over to it. I wasn't sure who the woman was, but she was tanned all over, flatness was on display, and her blond ponytail was scraggly. Was she cute? Yes, she was, but I was observing the things that I could complain about first. If they were a couple, they meshed pretty well together.

I put an array of fruit on my plate, and when I turned to take a glance at him, I bit into a juicy strawberry. His eyes connected with mine, and I sucked the strawberry juices from my finger.

"Delicious," I whispered, then turned my head. I sorted through more of the fruit, and when I inhaled the addictive cologne, I looked beside me. There stood Mr. Gorgeous. A plate was in his hand, and as we went for the same utensil to pick up the cantaloupe, he invited me to go ahead.

"No, after you. I think I already have enough on my plate."

"I hope not," he said. "What's your name?"

"Chase." If you knew me, you knew I didn't waste much time going after what I wanted. "Is that your wife you're with?"

"No, but a companion."

"Too bad. Not like I care either way, just thought I may have been on to something." I walked away and heard him say, "Maybe so."

I was too giddy going to meet up with Veronica and A.J. They seemed to be deep in conversation and were laughing loudly. I sat at the table, and A.J. stood up, asking Veronica if she wanted anything else before he left. She looked at her almost empty plate.

"No, I'm good, but thanks for asking."

"All right. I'm going to let you have some time with your friend, but I will definitely see you later."

"No doubt." She smiled as he walked away.

I set my tray on the table. "Oh, look at your hot self. I must be rubbing off on you."

"Maybe." She blushed. "But we won't be banging any headboards against the wall tonight. I hope that's not what he's thinking, but it was good to talk to him. He seems pretty cool. He lives in Chicago and you know that's just right around the corner from St. Louis."

"Did the two of you exchange phone numbers?"

"Yes. I'll see what's up with him, but I really came here to chill and have a good time."

"I feel you on that. And, by the way, you remember that man with the green eyes from last night, don't you?"

"How could I forget?"

"Well, I saw him in there eating breakfast with Barbie. I got his attention, and I think I may be on to something."

Veronica's smile widened. "For real? Girl, you'd better eat him alive. There's no doubt in my mind that you will, but in the meantime, I'm here to have fun and I'm not thinking about no man! Let's get off this ship and go see what all this paradise around us is about!"

I quickly finished my breakfast, and as soon as Veronica and I left the ship, she spotted David Beckham's look, alike and his companion. Veronica nudged my side and I noticed the two of them holding hands. *How cute,* I thought. *Maybe I should back off of him and forget about it.* For the moment, I did.

We hit the shops on the island, buying everything from seashells to sunglasses. Veronica bought some T-shirts for her daughter, and picked out a handmade necklace and straw purse for her daughter as well. Since Lance had been so nice to me, I bought him a pair of glasses and a T-shirt. I wanted to ask if he wanted to go with us, but he was always playing so broke. We spent about three to four hours shopping, then were ready to go on a tour. A black man in a taxi van drove us around the island, telling us about the Bahamas history. He drove us to Paradise Island, where we got a chance to see the inside of the Atlantis hotel. It was amazingly beautiful, and the thing that impressed me the most was the huge aquarium inside of the hotel. The hotel itself was awesome, and my camera was flashing away. I even snapped a shot of Mr. Sexy, as I saw him leaning against a wall near the exit. His cargo pants were rolled up underneath his knees, showing his tanned calves and brown leather sandals. His T-shirt rested on his muscles, and when he saw me flash the picture, he winked at me. That man had no idea how much trouble he was about to find himself in, and I kept thinking about how and when I was going to make it happen. This was only a four-day, three-night vacation, and I was already on day two.

Veronica snatched the camera from my hand. "She saw you take that picture," Veronica said, eyeballing the companion. I knew she did, but I knew she wasn't tripping off me when he had other eyes on him as well.

"Get your panties out of your butt," I said. "That woman has confidence written all over her, and the last thing she thinks is that her man can be coaxed by a woman like me, especially a black woman. Now, give me my camera back and let's go out to the pool area to take some pictures."

We left to go take pictures, checked out the casino, and walked around for at least another hour. As we were making our way back to the taxi van, someone tapped my shoulder.

"Excuse me, ma'am," he said. "You dropped some-thing."

Mr. Sexy gave me a piece of paper, and walked off with his companion. Veronica was squeezing her fists together, squealing at the same time. She looked like a kid in a candy store, telling me to read the note. I didn't, until we were on the van and seated.

It read: *What is your cabin number? By the way, my name is Steve.* Veronica cracked up and I tossed the paper over my shoulder.

"What the fu—"

Out of all the names he could have had, why did his name have to be Steve?

"Well, at least it ain't Steven, or Stevie," she said.

I cut my eyes at her, thinking about how quickly my anticipation had faded away.

We were back on the ship by 6:00 P.M., getting ready for dinner. I wanted to be comfortable, so I wore a black bell-sleeve stretch dress that cut across my chest, leaving one shoulder bare. It was short and went well with my silver strapped heels and silver accessories. My earrings dangled from my earlobes and my hair was up in a bun. I added fluff to my bangs, and I felt extremely pleased about the way I looked.

Veronica looked nice too. The red dress she wore stopped slightly above her knees and had gemstones around the neckline. Her makeup was just right and her hair was combed back, but flipped at the ends. We were seated at the dinner table with three other couples, and everyone was inquiring about each other. Me being me, my eyes scanned the room, looking for one person in particular. When I spotted him, my thoughts about not responding to his note went out the window. I figured he could wear the hell out of a single-breasted black suit, but damn! Did he have to do it like that? He was smiling and talking to the people at his table, but didn't notice me. I wrote on the napkin in front of me, then told Veronica I would be right back.

As I walked past his table to go to the ladies' room, I eyeballed him. He saw me and I turned my head. I went into the ladies' room for a few minutes, checking myself in the mirror. A few minutes later, Steve's woman walked in, standing next to me. She looked at herself in the mirror, glossing her lips. I wasn't sure what was up, until she cleared her throat.

"Don't even think about it," she said, looking at me in the mirror. "He is off limits."

I turned to her, just so we could be face-to-face. The one thing I hated was to be confronted by another woman, and that made my pursuit of her man even stronger.

"I can think whatever I want, and unless he tells me that he's off limits, what you say doesn't matter. Just so you know, I took this trip to have a good time. I intend to do just that, and if your man can enhance my vacation in any way, I'm all for it."

I stepped away from the mirror and she reached for my arm, pressing into it with her nails. Before I knew it, I had a grip on the back of her hair, and had backed her up to the wall. I jerked her head, causing her to squeeze her eyes.

"Don't put your fucking hands on me, bitch. If you are that worried about me, then I suggest you go somewhere and have a serious talk with your man. Because if he shows up at my cabin tonight, I am going to fuck his brains out and give him something that he'll never forget."

I pushed her head aside, and listened to her rant on my way out the door.

As soon as I came out of the bathroom, I saw Steve standing by the men's restroom. I gave him the napkin and walked off.

"Hey," he said. I turned. "You look awesome."

I winked. "I know. So do you."

I went back to my seat, watching Steve and his woman dispute with each other from a distance. My note asked him to someway or somehow meet me on the top deck after dinner. I wasn't going to give him my cabin number yet, because I had to make sure his head was on straight. I damn sure didn't want anyone to find me in the morning with my head chopped off, or my body thrown into the ocean. I could tell a little something about a person just through conversation, so I hoped he'd find a way to meet me.

Dinner was just okay for me. I didn't know if it was really the food, or that I was thinking about what had happened in the bathroom. The nerve of that trick putting her hands on me. She should have known better, stepping to me like that. Her actions infuriated me, but I kept my cool. I kept running my mouth with the people at the table, and at least the dessert was good. I whispered to Veronica that I was going to the upper level after dinner, and since she told me that she and A.J. were going to check out one of the shows on the island, that made it easier for me to slip away. I advised her to be careful, and she suggested the same.

After dinner, I climbed the stairs to the upper level, standing close to the edge to peer over the railing. It was a long way down, but the scenery was irresistible. I wondered if I could live like this, every day, for the rest of my life. The people on the island were so nice, and something about the whole thing made me feel as if home didn't even exist. As I was deep in thought, I heard footsteps on the wood flooring. Steve had a glass of something in his hand, and he smiled as he walked toward me. He leaned against the rail in front of me and faced me.

"Are you going on the island tonight? You know, most people are on the island and you should be too," he said.

"I'm going. How about you?"

"I'm going too, but I'm more concerned about what I'll be doing when I get back."

"Yeah, I was thinking about that too. Do you have anything in mind?"

"I sure do." He smiled and sipped from his glass of alcohol. "But I can show you better than I can tell you."

"What about your companion? Is she going to be a problem?"

"If she's not a problem for you, then she won't be one for me. You let me worry about her. All you have to do is provide me with a time and your cabin number."

"I promise to do more than that, but for starters, I'll see you at two. My cabin number is 13B."

He took another sip from his drink, gazing at me with those pretty olive green eyes. "Can I bring you anything? You know, something to drink . . ."

"No, just bring me something to play with. I'm sure you know what that is."

He was even sexier when he blushed. "I do."

Steve told me he'd see me later, and I watched as he walked off. The backside of him was finger-licking good, and it was a toss-up between the back and front of him. Either way, I couldn't go wrong with this one. I had to be the luckiest bitch, whore, slut, woman—or whatever you'd wish to call me—in the entire world. Damn, I loved my life and felt free to do whatever I wished.

I hooked up with Veronica and A.J. on the island and we sat around listening to several men beating on drums, making their own music. We ordered conch from a food shack and I was surprised that it was pretty good. I washed it down with Kalik beer, which the people around us recommended, and I had some wine coolers, too. Around a quarter to two, we headed back to the ship. Veronica surprised me when she did not let A.J. come into her room. He didn't push, either. I was so proud of the changes she'd made in her life. Maybe some of her good habits would rub off on me. I looked forward to a long friendship with her, but at the end of the day, I was living my life how Chase Jenkins chose to. A.J. told Veronica he'd see her tomorrow, and we all looked forward to our day at sea.

For now, I knew what I was about to get myself into, and believe it or not, I was tired as ever. I sat on the bed in my cabin, taking off my heels. I had been in them all night, and should have known better. My feet were sore, and I rubbed my achy feet. I dropped back on the bed for a minute, then sat up to pull off my dress. I didn't have on a bra, but I remained on the bed in my lime green lace panties. There was a knock at the door, so I tossed my dress in the chair. I slowly opened the door, and when I peeked to see who it was, I saw Steve. His eyes were glassy, but still addictive. I could tell he'd had more alcohol, and the smell of it entered the cabin with him. He wasted no time wrapping his arms around my body, and my bare breasts squeezed against his solid rock–carved chest. His tongue went into my mouth, and thus far, this was working for me well. He backed me up to the bed, assisting me with ripping his shirt open.

With each second that passed, things got more intense. He tugged at my panties, tearing them away from my brown skin. Before I could even get at the button on his pants, his fingers stroked my slit like a violin, and he pushed them into me. I gasped, while sucking his soft and juicy-ass lips. My hands were squeezing his chest, and I was so excited about the rotations of his fingers that I let him work with his pants and a condom.

After soaking me with his fingers, he finally removed his pants and placed on a condom. His dick was doable, so I got hyped. When he lay on top of me, oh, my God! His body was jaw dropping and all I could do was enjoy the feel of it. My hands were roaming everywhere and I couldn't stop kissing him, I was just that pleased. I wrapped my legs around his back while he worked magic with my titties. The arch in my back had already formed, and he lifted one of my legs onto his shoulder. I felt his dick enter me, but as he started to stroke me, my eyes popped open. I couldn't feel a thing, and was mad about it, too. Maybe he had gone down or something, but as he kept on stroking, I wasn't really sure.

"Ahh," he softly said in my ear, wetting it with his tongue. "This is good. Your insides feel so good."

It was good to know that one of us was pleased, but in an effort not to disappoint, I kept up my rhythm. Maybe it was the position that we were in. I wanted so badly for this to work. I squeezed my fist, slamming it onto the bed. I'm sure he thought I was about to have an orgasm, but that simply was not the case. My legs dropped from his waist, and I whispered to him that I wanted to turn around on my stomach. He eased out of me, and I at least felt when he did that. Yep, there was something inside of me, but before I rolled over, I looked down to be sure. His dick was very hard, and the length of it was fair. I smiled, thinking that I had just been too spoiled by Steven, and it was hard for any man to compete with him. Steve kissed my shoulders and his lips pecked down my back. His tongue scrolled across my butt, and he sucked chunks of it into his mouth. He bit that sucker, too, but his bites were arousing. He massaged it real well, and was complimenting me as he did it.

"Nice. Oh, so damn plump and nice," he said.

Compared to that flatness he was with, I was sure this was quite a change. I was ready for the dick treatment again, so I reached back to touch it. It was slippery, but hard. Steve lay over me, and we both put his thing inside of me. Almost immediately, I wanted to give up. But as he got his rhythm going, it got a little better. Why? Because I had already kicked in Plan B, and that was to envision Steven's long black pipe sliding in and out of me instead. This made me even more anxious for Steve. By all means, nothing against white men, and the passion was very much appreciated. But I would take a big black dick any day over this. When it was all said and done, it was obvious why some black women weren't willing to give up on their black men.

Steve crept out of my cabin at almost four o'clock in the morning. I basically worked with what I had, and on a scale from one to ten, I gave it a seven. I could tell he'd put forth his best effort, and I had to give credit to a man who could suck breasts well and touch my body in the right places. Like I said, I had had some top dogs in my life, and I knew how difficult it was to please me. To at least get a seven out of me, Steve should have considered himself victorious.

We spent the entire Sunday at sea, and every time I saw Steve, I purposely swooped in another direction. Veronica was laughing her butt off, as I had told her about last night's events. We sat around watching one of the waiters carve ice, and then the crew started to play games with the people on board. I didn't feel like playing games, and since it was my last full day on the ship, I went to the top level to relax in my bikini. A.J. and Veronica stayed to play games. I was happy that she was enjoying herself so much.

I lay on a towel on the lounging chair, resting on my stomach. I'd already seen the same four brothers checking me out, and as soon as one of them approached me, I stuck with my lie.

"Hey, pretty lady, where your man at?"

I sat up and peered over the rail to look down below. I pointed to A.J. and Veronica. "There. Right there."

"You can do so much better," he said, cocky as ever. "That dude don't have nothing on me."

"I'm not talking about the man. I'm talking about the woman. I don't date men, sorry."

"Like I said, you still can do better. How about you and me hooking up later?"

Oh no, he didn't just go off on my friend. "How about we don't. You're not my type, and I don't like men who come off as being arrogant."

"And I'm not a fan of women with smart mouths. Enjoy your day, all right?"

He walked away and I got comfortable again on the lounge chair, hoping that no one else would bother me. For a while, I was at peace. But as soon as the lady next to me moved, Steve came over and laid his towel on the chair next to me. He only had on swimming trunks, and he relaxed on his stomach like me.

"Did you get any rest after last night?" he asked.

"Not much. I will turn in early tonight, though, and that is a guarantee."

"I don't think I've had more than two or three hours of sleep since I've been here. I'll sleep when I get home. I'm slightly disappointed that my vacation is almost over."

"Me too. I really had a good time, and I so look forward to doing this again in the near future."

"Where do you live?"

"In St. Louis. I'm a long way from home. How about you?"

"California."

"I figured that. Do you model or something? You are really a nice-looking man, and I assume you're into something like that."

"As a matter of fact, I am. What kinds of magazines do you subscribe to?"

"*Ebony, Jet, Essence . . .*"

He chuckled. "No, you won't find me in those magazines. Do me a favor. Give me your address and I'll mail my magazines to you."

"Why can't you tell me so I can just purchase them?"

"Because I want to surprise you."

"Okay. I'll write down my address and give it to you."

"When?"

I smiled, looking into those eyes that I most likely would never see after my cruise. "When you come to my room tonight. Make it earlier this time; that's if you don't mind finishing what we started."

"I would like that. So glad you asked."

I wasn't sure if or when Steven would get his act together at home, so I had to get myself on full for a while. Who better to do it with than this fine mofo? At the moment, I really couldn't think of anyone else.

Chapter 12

Coming back home from a vacation like that was tough. And heading back to work on Monday was even tougher. I couldn't believe how discouraged I was, but I made a promise to myself to take vacations more often.

The one thing about my new job was that it was boring as hell. Josh really didn't require much of me like Liz did, and he was always sitting around running his mouth. I didn't mind talking, but I liked to keep myself busy so time would go by quickly. Having little to do made time go by at a slow pace. I knew this job wouldn't last for long. I also wanted a job that could challenge me, and, unfortunately, I didn't really see this going anywhere. It paid my bills, and that was it.

At this point in my life, that wasn't good enough. I had ambition, and I had always wanted to run a company or strive for the highest position in one. I had a bachelor's degree in business, but, as I said earlier, I had to settle for a job as a secretary. Years ago, I had a much better job working in upper management at a hospital, but that didn't go so well. Actually, that's where I'd met Drake, but in an effort not to conflict with him, I sought out other job opportunities. We saw each other so much at work, and both of us felt that we didn't need to work together, too. I now knew why he was against working with me, and I would put some money on it that he was dating other people at our job.

With me being around all the time, that was a setback for him. I was so over him, though, but the same couldn't be said for Steven. I checked my phone, surprised that he had called twice. I was too tired to return his phone call last night, but while I was at work, I called him. His voicemail came on, so I left a message, explaining that I had been on vacation and couldn't be reached. I let him know that I was back and told him to call me whenever he got time.

My phone call from Steven didn't come until I was at home, getting ready for bed. He asked if we could meet somewhere, so I suggested that we talk over dinner.

"No," he said. "I have a better idea. I'm going to be tied up this week, but on Saturday morning, meet me at the AMC movie theatres by your place around nine o'clock. I haven't been to the movies in a while, and I want to check out this new flick with Robert De Niro in it."

"Why so early? The movie theatre doesn't open up that early, does it?"

"Don't worry about that. Just meet me there. We'll talk then."

He sounded more upbeat since the last time we'd spoken, so I had to ask. "Have you forgiven me for interrupting your dinner? You sound as if you have."

"I said we'll talk. I'm not one to hold grudges, and

you already know how addicted to you I am, don't you?"

I didn't even respond. I told Steven I would see him soon, and was glad that he had come to his senses.

On Saturday, I got dressed and made my way to the AMC theatre that Steven mentioned. There were only a few cars parked on the lot, but I saw his black BMW. When I got inside, he was waiting for me in the lobby. He was indeed smiling, so that was a good thing.

"Do you want some popcorn and something to drink?"

"Sure," I said, especially since I hadn't eaten anything.

Steven got a big bucket of popcorn and both of us a soda. Afterward, we went into the movie theatre and sat by our lonesome selves.

"I still don't understand why we're here so early," I said, taking the soda from his hand.

"Because I wanted to be alone with you, and you know that I know too many people. You can rent these theatres for yourself, and that's what I chose to do."

"Well, thank you. And it's nice to be hanging out with you like this."

"I really don't mind doing this from time to time, and I suspect that you would like us to do this more often, right?"

"It doesn't matter to me. I'm fine with the situation. I know that our relationship has limitations."

"You say that, but that night at the restaurant, you were highly upset. I . . . I just don't want us to go down that road again. I like you a lot, Chase, but I need to know that you're the one who can handle this. I refuse to be with a woman who watches after me and questions me about my whereabouts.

"I already have to check in with Liz, and I shouldn't have to do that with you. It makes me uncomfortable, and the reason I gravitated to you so easily was because you seemed to be that kind of woman who understood me. I liked how confident you were, and you didn't seem like the kind of woman who would easily jump on an emotional rollercoaster. Are you still that kind of confident woman who swept me off my feet that day in my office, or are you changing up on me?"

"I understand all about the kind of man you are, and I have no problem being the confident woman you need me to be. My only problem with you has been honesty. I don't know why you told me you were going on a trip and didn't go, and I also don't know why you want me to believe that you rarely have sex with your wife. I know you do, and I expect you to. Does it bother me? Hell yeah, it does, but I'm well aware of what I got myself into. I can definitely handle this, and as long as you are truthful with me about where we stand, I'm good."

"I had to reschedule my trip and move it to a later date. It's as simple as that. I didn't feel it was necessary to call and let you know, unless we had plans. We didn't have any plans, so you didn't get a phone call. As far as sex with Liz, now, why should I have to go into details about that with you? That makes no sense at all, and how often we do it doesn't really matter. As long as you're getting what you want, why should you care? I'm not slacking on you, am I?"

"No. And you'd better not either."

Steven turned his head, puckering for a kiss. "I won't."

"Good. I assume we're back on then, right?"

"You got that right. And for a very long time, I hope."

"You'll have to get tired of me before I get tired of you."

"That may be awhile."

This time, I gave Steven a lengthier kiss. I was pleased we were moving in the right direction again, and in the direction that I wanted.

The movie screen started to show previews. I had finally dipped into the popcorn and playfully licked the butter from my fingers.

"You're a hot-ass something," Steven said. "And I hope you had fun with that Negro you took on vacation with you. Where did you go?"

"I went on a cruise with Veronica, and if you would have looked at your credit card statement, you would have known that. I assure you that I didn't go overboard with spending, but we had so much fun. I could have stayed there forever."

"I'll bet. Did you meet anybody?"

I poked him with my elbow. "Wouldn't you like to know? But let's just say that I met no one like you."

"Now, why doesn't that surprise me? I'm the one, and definitely the only."

He had that shit right; that's why I had to be careful. Something about this thing with Steven was starting to make me uncomfortable. I didn't want to get caught up with a married man, and whenever I could feel myself getting too close, it was time to back up. He was saying all of the right things, while at the same time showing me that he cared. There were little things, like what he had done today, that made me feel as if he needed this just as much as I did. A part of me even figured that I could get more out of him, but I didn't want to come across as being a mistress who was out to take everything that he had. That was in no way the case, but for the time being, a good conversation, good sex, and a good movie never hurt anyone.

Steven and I left the movie theatre, and we stood by his car discussing the next time we'd hook up. I couldn't take any more time off from work, and the earliest time I could see him in the morning would be on Friday.

"Nah, I don't want to wait that long," he said. "It's been awhile and I'm anxious. What about Monday or Tuesday after work? We can't do my house, so you may have to settle for a hotel."

"I'll settle for it this time, especially since I'm so anxious for you too. Until then, be good and I'll see you soon."

We shared an intense kiss and Steven got into his car. He sped off and I slowly walked to my car. The closer I got to it, I noticed a long, deep scratch on the side. The scratch was wavy and it cut into my burgundy paint job. I looked around, but saw no one in sight. Yeah, I was frustrated that somebody had turned the tables on me, but who in the hell was it? The only person I could think of was Liz. She was the only one who had a reason to do something like this, and it pretty much made sense. I just couldn't see her doing something this extreme, and even though she was no better than me, this kind of move did not fit her character. Just to be sure, I got inside my car and quickly called Steven.

"Say, baby. I'm sorry to bug you already, but where is Liz?"

"Why? I thought we just discussed this—"

"No, no . . . it's nothing like that. Somebody scratched my car and they scratched it up pretty good."

"What? I . . . I don't know who could have done something so silly, but I know for a fact it wasn't Liz. Trust me, if she had any idea about us, she would call me out immediately. Maybe somebody at the movie theatre did it to be funny."

"Maybe so."

"Call your insurance company and let them fix it. How much is your deductible?"

"Five hundred dollars."

"I'll take care of that for you. Just call and have it fixed."

"Thank you. And if you notice any changes in Liz, please, please let me know."

"I know my wife, and I assure you that she's good. If anything changes, you know I'll be in touch."

I ended our call, hoping that someone at the movie theatre had nothing else better to do. My car was parked a bit crookedly, so maybe the person next to me got upset because they had a hard time squeezing in. I wasn't sure, but I was definitely going to watch my back. I hadn't asked Veronica about Liz's behavior at work in a while, and I made a mental note to do so later.

I spoke to Veronica later that day, but she said that she hadn't noticed anything out of the ordinary with Liz. She said that Liz had already hired a new secretary, though, and another woman from a different department took over Claudette's position. I'd even thought about her scratching up my car, but how would she know I was at the movie theatres this morning? And, if she saw me with Steven for one second, she would run like a bat out of hell to tell Liz.

"Are you sure?" I asked Veronica again. "Has she

been in a good mood or bad one? She knows that the two of us hang together. Has she asked you anything about me?"

"No, she hasn't. She's really been nice, and to me, you know Liz has always been a nice person. Steven did come up here to take her to lunch this week, and they seemed as if everything was fine. She came back giddy as ever. As for me and Liz, you know the two of us have always gotten along well."

I hated to ask, but I had to. "You've never said anything to her about me and Steven, have you? I hate to ask, but I am a little worried about what happened to my car. The more I think about it, that scratch was done by someone who was angry."

"I swear to God that I haven't said a word. I hope you don't think I would put your business out there like that. After all that you've done for me, girl, I owe you big time. If Liz knows anything about you and Steven, she did not get it from me. I know her attitude would be way more off if she suspected her husband was cheating on her. I'm just not seeing it."

"Steven said the same thing. I guess I'm worrying for nothing. It's probably that old, stupid fool Drake trying to get me back for keying his car that day."

"I forgot you told me about that. Maybe so. Why don't you give him a call, just to see what's up with him? If he sounds bitter, then you know what's up."

I didn't think that was such a bad idea, so I called Drake. His number had been disconnected. I had no other way to reach him, so I sat for a minute thinking. I always appreciated Lance's opinion, and wanted to know his thoughts. I walked across the hall and knocked on his door. I could hear music coming from inside, and when he opened the door, light smoke came out.

"What are you in here burning up?" I asked.

"I'm frying a couple pieces of chicken. Do you want some?"

"No, thank you," I said, sitting on his couch.

I waited until he finished with his chicken to bother him about my issues. He finally came over to the couch to sit. The music was still so loud that I got up to turn it down.

"You know I'm mad at you," he said, biting into the chicken.

"Why? What did I do?"

"You went on your vacation without me. I talked to Veronica and she told me about the good time y'all had."

"Yeah, well, we did have a good time. At least I thought of you and brought you some things back, didn't I? I'm sorry I didn't ask you to go, but I didn't think you'd want to go with us."

"I'm over it. Besides, my funds are low and I couldn't afford a vacation right now if my life depended on it."

"I know how that is, but thanks to Steven for making it possible. The trip was so worth it, too."

"I'm glad you had a good time." He sipped from his glass, then bit into another piece of chicken like a pit bull, tearing at a piece of meat.

"Damn," I laughed. "Is it that good?"

"Delicious," he said, playfully putting the piece of chicken up to my mouth. "Here, take a bite."

I pushed the chicken away. It looked too greasy for me, but the potatoes on his plate looked good.

"So, tell me about your vacation," he said. "What did you do, other than fuck somebody?"

My mouth flew open. "Did Veronica tell you what I did? I can't believe she told you!"

"She didn't tell me nothing. You just did. I warned you about speaking before you think, and I was just playing with you when I said that."

I pushed Lance's shoulder. "I was just playing too, so there."

"No, you weren't. You know you let somebody get into those panties, and if that's how you're doing it, Ms. Jenkins, then go ahead and keep on doing you."

I pouted. "Are you disappointed in me?"

Lance held his fingers close together. "Just a little. Not a lot, but a little."

"Well, either way, the vacation was fun. We ate like pigs, we shopped, we danced, we went to Paradise Island, we saw the aquarium, we lay out in the sun, we took a lot of pictures, and, oh yeah, did I tell you we ate like pigs?"

"Sounds like fun." Lance covered his mouth and belched. "Excuse me. Sorry about that, but you just don't know what you're missing."

"Oh, yes, I do. Anyhow, I need to ask you something."

"What? I'm listening."

I told Lance about the incident that happened today, and updated him on my possible suspects. I had even thrown Korey in there, simply because I hadn't spoken to him in quite some time and I didn't know where his head was either.

Lance wasted no time canceling out everyone I had mentioned, with the exception of Liz.

"If you're asking me who scratched your car, your answer is Liz."

"Now, why would she do something stupid like that? I don't have no beef with her."

Lance cocked his head back. "Duh. In case you forgot, you're fucking her husband. You may not have no beef with her, but she damn sure got beef with you. If you don't think she knows about you and Steven, you're crazy. Most married women know about their husbands' mistresses, trust me."

"It's not her," I whined. "She's just not that kind of woman, so it has to be someone else. If you knew her like I did, you would know that she would go to Steven first. She couldn't care less about me, and it would be a total embarrassment for her to confront me about this."

"That's why she's not. I would put some money on it that Liz knows about you and Steven, but she's not saying anything."

"Why wouldn't she? When I caught Drake cheating on me, I took immediate action. Why wait for months and months to confront somebody? That doesn't make sense. That's why I know it's not her."

"Hey, you asked for my opinion and I told you. I could be wrong, but you know how y'all women do it."

"I absolutely do. And women get on it, right away. Somebody else scratched my car, and when I find out who it was, their tail is mud."

"Could it possibly be that you're blowing this out of proportion? You got a few scratches on your car, and now you think somebody's out to get you."

"You think so, huh? Well, when you get finished licking your fingers, go outside and look at my car. Tell me what you think. I've scratched up plenty of cars in my day, and I can pretty much tell when there is anger behind those scratches or someone just doing it to be mean. I don't think the latter is the case."

Lance stepped over me and went outside for a few minutes. He came back, closing the door behind him. He sat on the couch, and without saying anything, he sipped from his glass.

"Ah," he said, clearing his throat. "Now that quenched my thirst right there."

I laughed and removed the glass from his hand. "Would you stop playing? You saw it, didn't you? What do you think?"

"I already told you what I think. It's Liz and that's all there is to it."

I cut my eyes at Lance. He didn't know Liz like I did, but just to be sure, I was going to have lunch with Veronica on Monday. I was going to the office to pick her up, and hopefully I'd get a chance to see Liz face-to-face.

When Monday came, I stopped by my old job and went to the department where I used to work. I had already asked Veronica if Liz was there, and Veronica said that she was. Before going into her office to speak, I stood with Veronica at her cubicle.

"How has she been acting today?" I whispered.

"Normal. I don't know why you're even worried about it. I don't care what Lance says, Liz doesn't have a clue."

"Wish me luck," I said, heading to her office. The door was already open, but she was looking down at some papers in front of her. I knocked so she would look up. When she did, she didn't even smile.

"Hello, Liz," I said. "I came here to have lunch with Veronica, but I wanted to stop in to say hello."

She removed her glasses and invited me into her office. "Thanks for stopping in. I'm glad that you did. If you have a minute to spare, sit down, I want to talk to you about something."

I was a little nervous, but if this bitch put her hands on me, it was going to be on. I sat in the chair in front of her.

"Listen," she said, clenching her hands together. "I wanted to apologize to you about what happened here the day you got fired. I thought long and hard about that day, Chase, and I struggled with whether I made the right decision. You had always given me your best, and I know how difficult it was for you to deal with some of the things Claudette said to you. I spoke to some of the other supervisors about it, and a few of them told me that I shouldn't have fired you.

"Let me be clear: I did not think it was right for you to involve yourself with Claudette's fiancé, but you were correct when you said it was your personal business. It was, and again, I apologize for the decision I made that day. I hope that you can forgive me. It would truly mean a lot to me if you would at least consider it."

I was really worried now, simply because I now knew somebody else was fucking with me. I had too many haters to really think about who, but I had to cross Liz off my list. "It's no big deal, Liz. I found another job and I've moved on from this. As you said, you had to do what you felt was necessary that day. Claudette's time was coming to an end anyway, and I'm just glad that you got a chance to see her for the person she really was."

Liz chuckled. "It took me a while, but I did. I'd been under so much pressure from Mr. Aimes, and I couldn't afford for him to keep coming down on my back. I'm glad you understand, and I really do wish you all the best. If you ever need to use me for a reference, please do."

Liz stood up, and reached out to give me a hug. As we hugged, I felt a tad bit bad about what Steven and I were doing behind her back. Then again, sometimes it happened to the best of us. Too bad.

After I left Liz's office, Veronica and I had lunch. She felt as if Claudette was the one who had scratched my car, and I, myself, felt it was time to pay her a visit.

Later that day, I followed Claudette and her man to his house. Since I figured she'd been keeping her eyes on me, I wanted to see what she'd been up to as well. They left her house, and parked in the parking lot of his apartment complex. I expected him to get out of the car and go about his business, but that didn't happen. They sat in her car kissing for a while, and then she got out with him. Walking hand in hand to his door, I watched as they went inside. I'd thought about waiting until she came out, but there was no telling how long I'd be sitting. I had to come up with something fast, and put her on the spot so she'd admit to scratching my car.

I walked to her boyfriend's door, and when I placed my ear on it, I could hear Claudette's moans coming through the door. Luckily, her man was in no way attractive to me, 'cause if he was, it would be on. I'd thought about knocking, but there was always an easy way to maneuver a door. I used my ATM card, sliding it into the crack of the door, particularly in front of the lock. The card was thin enough to move the lock aside, and low and behold, the door popped open. I quietly widened the door, then closed it behind me. The bedroom was only several feet away, and as I tiptoed my way to it, I was so disturbed by what I saw inside.

Claudette was straddling her man's lap, moving nothing but her shoulders and hair. She was causing all of this ruckus and wasn't doing a damn thing. At least her man was trying to pump something into her, but even he had a look of frustration on his face. He was silent as ever and his eyes were closed. Obviously, he was thinking of someone else. I wanted to go and push that bitch aside, just to show her how to really ride a man. And after standing for another two minutes, I couldn't take it anymore. I removed my skirt, but left on my turquoise thong. My blouse stayed on too, and so did my high-heeled shoes, just in case I had to make a swift exit. A tiny silver hand pistol was inside my shirt pocket, just in case I needed it. I walked over to the bed, and as soon as I got on top of it, her man opened his eyes and Claudette snapped her head to the side.

"What in the fuck are you doing?" she spat with bugged eyes.

I gave her a hard shove, pushing her off her man's lap. She fell off the bed, and slammed into the wall. Her man quickly sat up, stunned by my presence.

"I didn't mean to interrupt," I said, calmly straddling his lap. His eyes were focused between my legs, hoping, I assumed, that I would remove my thong. "But I came here to talk to Claudette about something. I just happened to see that her performance was severely lacking, and I wanted to show her how to prevent her man from seeking satisfaction from a coworker." I rubbed his chest, and he didn't say a word. Claudette started to get up from the floor, but I gave her a devious look. I removed the pistol from my shirt, placing it next to me.

"Just chill and relax for a minute." I started to roll myself on top of her man, putting my hips and curvy backside into motion. "See, girl, you gotta stroke him like this. With every stroke, put an arch in your back to help with your rhythm. Don't be all stiff, and if you need to lean back on your hands for leverage, go ahead and do it. See," I said, placing my hands behind me. My legs were wide open for her man to see between them. I kept moving my hips in a circular motion, and looked at Claudette with her mouth hanging wide open.

"Are you ready to try this now? He got a pretty big dick, but if a man's dick keep flopping out of you while you're on top of him doing this, you may want to find another one. I understand if you want to take it slow, but just don't waste his time. He deserves to be inside of a woman who knows what she's doing." I looked at him. "Right?"

He slowly nodded, but still looked to be in disbelief. I got off his lap, and slapped my ass to make it jiggle. "If she doesn't get her shit together, call me. There are plenty of women willing to do the right thing, and I'm one of them." I picked up the gun next to me. It wasn't loaded, but I figured it was needed in order for Claudette to tell me the truth. I aimed it at her.

"You can stand up now, and when you open your mouth, I want the truth."

She slowly eased off the floor, but with attitude. Her twisted mouth was bound to get her smacked, and I hoped she knew that.

"Why did you mess with my car?" I asked.

Her neck was already starting to turn. "What are you talking about? I didn't—"

I grabbed her by her hair, and shoved her onto the bed. I aimed the gun at her again, this time cocking it.

She panicked and scooted next to her man. He pushed her away. "Shit, you'd better move and tell her the truth. If not, I will."

"So, so I scratched your car," she said. "You know I'm still upset with you about Korey. What you did to me was wrong! Dead wrong!"

"Fuck you and fuck Korey too. You are going to pay me for my car, and when I send you the entire bill, I'm giving you a week to pay it. If you do not, that will only mean trouble for you. I don't have to tell you what kind of trouble, and if you think I'm playing, I dare you to try me."

"I'll send your freaking money to you, but I want you to leave. Leave me the hell alone and don't ever come around me again."

"Watch your mouth. And since it's running so much, I assume you've told Liz why I was at the movies that day, right?"

"I haven't told Liz anything, and I'm glad you're fucking her husband. If she wouldn't have fired me, I would tell her every single thing I know. So have fun with him, and all of you crazy-ass people can go to hell. Just leave me alone! Please!"

At this point, I didn't care if Claudette told Liz or not. I'd have to answer to her sooner or later, and Steven did too. I put my skirt back on, and after I gave Claudette's man my phone number to reach me, I left.

I was horny as hell, so I called Steven to make arrangements to hook up. He told me he'd be off by seven, no later than eight. But when I called his office, he was still there. I was already at the hotel waiting for him, and I asked what time he thought he could make it.

"Give me about another hour, maybe hour and a half. I will get there as soon as I can, and do not take your sweet self home."

"I won't. Just hurry."

"I'm doing my best."

I hung up, feeling disappointed that he was tied up at work. It had been several weeks since we'd been together sexually, and he had already broken our agreement about me getting it at least three times a week. Besides, after my experience on the cruise, I was ready for some real meat. I quickly covered myself with a cotton robe and slid into my sandals. I drove to Steven's office, and saw his car parked in the parking lot with several others. Steven always told me to park around back, so I did. I wasn't sure if anyone else was in the office with him. I didn't see anyone, but when I looked inside, the lights were on in some of the offices. The doors to the lobby stayed open until ten o'clock, so I went inside, going directly to Steven's office. His door was open, and like always, he was leaned back in the chair with papers in his hand. I cleared my throat and he lifted his head.

"Woman, you are so darn hardheaded, aren't you?"

"About what? Instead of taking my sweet self home, I came here." I opened my robe, revealing a sliver of my nakedness underneath. "I was getting so bored at the hotel, and by the time you got there, I figured I'd be asleep."

I closed his door and slowly walked over to him. I sat on top of his desk, and he laid his papers next to me. His eyes scanned down my body and he rose up, standing directly in front of me.

"You are so damn sexy," he said, easing his hands inside of my robe to feel my naked body. Our lips met up, and it felt so magnificent to taste his tongue again. He removed the robe from my shoulders and placed tender kisses on my chest.

"Mmm, you smell delicious. I got a feeling that this pussy is going to feel spectacular to me tonight."

"I got you covered."

I started to remove Steven's tie, but when we saw headlights shining through from outside, Steven stepped away to peek out of his blinds. His head jerked back.

"Uh, that's Liz's car. I told—"

Before he could say anything else, I hurried off his desk and closed the robe in front of me. It was too late for me to run out of his office, so I switched to Plan B. The only place I could go was underneath his desk. My forehead was starting to sweat and my heart was racing fast. Steven was squeezing his forehead, and he quickly plopped down in his chair to calm his nerves. He scooted his chair up to his desk and I could hear something like a pen tapping on his desk. A few minutes later, a knock was on the door and Liz opened it.

"Hey, baby," Steven said. "What are you doing here?"

"I wanted to surprise you with something to eat. When we talked earlier, you sounded exhausted, and I knew you hadn't had anything to eat."

"Thank you. That was so sweet of you."

I assumed she was coming closer because Steven scooted further in to his desk. I could see a shadow of her heels in front of his desk, and it sounded as if she put something on top of it. Steven slightly lifted himself from his seat, and that's when I heard a tiny kiss. I heard movement, and I could tell Liz had taken a seat. Steven adjusted himself in the chair, then scooted into the desk again. I had a wonderful view from underneath his desk. Even his shiny black expensive leather shoes turned me on.

"How much longer are you going to be?" Liz asked.

"At least another hour or two. Go ahead and go home. I'll meet you there. If you stay here, you know I won't get anything done."

"I promise not to mess with you, even though I have a difficult time restraining myself around you."

Hell, she wasn't the only one. I definitely knew how she felt. I had already started to rub my hands on Steven's legs, and when I touched between them, his leg movements stopped. I touched his dick and started massaging it.

"It's difficult for me to restrain myself too," he said. "But I've got to get this work done. I'm meeting with my client first thing tomorrow morning. Give me about an hour, and I will do my best to hurry home."

"I'll have your bathwater waiting. One hour, Steven, and let this job go. You and I both have got to stop giving so much of ourselves to our careers. I would love to take a vacation with you soon. Let's plan to do so very soon, okay?"

"We will. I know exactly how you feel. We do need some time for ourselves."

"I agree."

I heard movement, and could hear Liz's heels on the floor. I figured she was walking to the door.

"Liz," Steven said.

"Yes."

"I love you."

"I love you too, honey. See you at home."

The sounds of her heels faded. Steven backed away from his desk, but told me not to move yet. He peeked through his blinds, and when the headlights went away, he stood up. I came from underneath the desk, and had never seen him look so flustered. He rubbed his face.

"Listen. I'll give you a call later this week. If I don't get home in an hour, she may get suspicious."

"And? I'm sorry to hear that. If you have only an hour, then I recommend that you spend your time wisely. You know how to do that, don't you?"

Steven stood for a moment, debating with himself and the time. I already knew what his decision would be, and when he removed his tie, I awaited him on the couch. We in no way wrapped it up in an hour, and after two long hours, I was sure when he got home he would have some explaining to do. If only I could be a fly on the wall.

Chapter 13

For the next two weeks, I was without Steven. We talked on the phone, but he had one excuse after another as to why we couldn't get together. The average person would have sweated him to death, or probably cried because she felt kicked to the curb or disrespected by his actions. An argument was bound to happen, but he wasn't getting any arguments from me. I in no way showed insecurities, and that caused Steven to kiss my butt. Plan B was to cancel him soon and find myself another man, but I wasn't quite ready to do that yet. He had sent me the money to get my car fixed, and I came out ahead when Claudette had sent her money too. Steven had even sent me some roses with a card attached, apologizing for our sudden setback that he promised to soon correct. I knew that it wasn't his fault that Liz was being a burden, and damn her for interrupting us that day. I could feel the intensity in my bones for him, and the cravings I had for him were like being addicted to crack. Well, maybe not crack, let's just be a bit more sensible and say chocolate.

When Steven called and told me Liz was finally taking her business trip, I was in a forgiving mood. According to him, she would be gone from Thursday to Sunday. I had already started to plan out each day, and Steven told me that we could do anything I wanted. Whatever it was, he said that he was down with it. All I wanted to do was let him hold me throughout the night, place gentle kisses on my forehead, wash me in the shower, bring me breakfast in bed . . . Okay, so I was lying. What I really wanted was to feel him inside of me, and as long as he was doing that, I was fine.

As expected, the week dragged on. I did get a surprise in the mail this week, and when I saw Steve's name on the envelope, I couldn't wait to see what was inside. It was the magazines that he had sent me, and on the cover of a well-known explicit magazine was a body shot of him sprawled out on the cover. I couldn't wait to look through the pictures inside, and grinned my butt off while flipping through them one by one. Steve was definitely the sexiest man alive. The other magazine wasn't so explicit. It was a men's clothing magazine, but in each picture his carved chest was showing and the clothes he wore were pretty costly. I felt so lucky to have shared those two nights with him, and even though they weren't everything that I wanted them to be, it was something I'd never forget. I kept the magazines on my coffee table, and couldn't wait to show them to Veronica or anyone else who wanted to see them.

Finally, according to Steven, Liz was gone and I could come right on over. I took an overnight bag with me, and stuffed it with several sexy pieces of lingerie and some casual clothes. Within the hour, I was at Steven's house, parking my car far down the street. I knocked on the door, and the moment he opened it, the adventure was on. We kissed our way up the steps, and as Steven removed my clothes on the way up, he playfully tossed them in the air, causing them to drop in the foyer. He couldn't wait to get me in his bed, and the thick comforter and silk sheets felt magnificent against my skin. I surely felt at home. I made a mental note to ask Liz where in the hell she'd gotten the mattress and just what kind it was. I fell back on the bed, and my head sunk into the plush soft pillows. Steven was already down low, tasting my sweetness. I closed my eyes, telling him how much I enjoyed these intense and risky moments with him. He couldn't even respond; all he could do was nod.

Now that I was at Steven's house with him, time wanted to move by quickly. I cuddled in bed with him last night, and slept like a baby as he secured me in his arms. Liz had called to let Steven know she'd made it to her destination. He had even chatted with her through his video Web camera and microphone, with his laptop resting on his chest. He was flat on his back, and he looked at her as she complained to him about being in a crappy hotel room. I was out of the laptop's view, but was giving him pleasure with my mouth, underneath the sheets. He quickly wrapped up his conversation with her, and we were already on day number two.

The day started with breakfast in bed. I told Steven to stay put, and went into the kitchen to whip up something. It wasn't much, but a bowl of cereal, some toast, and orange juice suited us just fine. I was impressed by how well Liz kept her kitchen. Everything was in place, and she was one very organized woman. The whole kitchen was spotless, and after I got finished with our breakfast, I was sure to put her kitchen back to the condition in which she'd had it. That was the least I could do for her.

I carried the tray upstairs and gave Steven his plate. While lying sideways on the bed with my clothes off, I put my plate in front of me. Steven, however, sat against the headboard.

"Why you burn my toast?" he asked, turning it over. I laughed because I thought the toast was a bit crisp.

"See, what happened was . . . That toaster was kind of tricky. I set the timer, but it didn't flip up the toast when I expected it to."

Steven smacked my butt, and put his plate aside to get after me. He lay on my backside, while pecking my shoulders.

"Are you having yourself a good time?" he asked.

I rolled on my back, just so I could look into his eyes. He cradled me underneath him. "I'm having a superb time. Thank you for making this happen. I appreciate your efforts."

"You'd better," he said. "And it only gets better from here."

I doubted that, simply because all good things come to an end. After we ate breakfast, Steven told me to chill out for a while and make myself at home. Since it was Friday, he said that he had to go to his office in the basement to handle a few things. He promised not to be long, and in his absence, I got comfortable in bed. I watched two of my favorite soap operas that I hadn't seen in a long time, and checked out a few reruns of some reality TV shows.

After a while, I started to get bored, so I went downstairs to find Steven. He was typing on his laptop computer, while sitting at his desk. I wrapped my arms around his neck, rubbing his chest.

"You really are all work and no play. I don't think I could ever be married to you because you work too much for me."

"Working is the key to making money. I gotta make money, don't I? Especially living in this kind of house."

"I know, but I'm getting so bored. I wanted to watch a movie with you, and didn't you tell me the other day that you could do a better job shaving me?"

Steven chuckled, and I thought about what led to us having that conversation. He said that he liked my coochie shaved bald, but I said that I liked it trimmed. I told him that if he wanted it that way, then he'd have to do it himself.

"You're not going to let me get any work done this weekend, are you?"

"No. None. This is a very rare occasion and we really need to take advantage of it."

Steven followed me upstairs to the master bathroom.

"Sit between the Jack and Jill sinks," he ordered. "Let me have some for-real fun."

He sat in front of me, then opened a drawer next to him. Inside were a new pack of razors and he placed them on the counter. He got a thick towel and laid it on the counter as well. He looked between my legs and rubbed his hands together.

"Wait a minute," I said. "What if you cut me? I'm nervous about this. My stuff is already shaved enough."

"If I cut you, I'll suck your blood. I love the way you have it trimmed, I just want to see what it looks like all shaved off."

I bravely opened my legs wider.

Steven snapped his fingers. "Shit, I almost forgot. Don't move. I'll be right back."

He left the bathroom, and came back moments later with a whipped cream container in his hand. I cracked up, as he was so very creative. He shook the container and sat back in the chair. As he covered my pussy with the new form of shaving cream, it was awfully cold. He spread the cream with his fingers, then licked off the leftovers. When he picked up the razor, I had an unsure look on my face.

"Relax," he said. "I got this."

I looked down and watched as he carefully slid the blade over my goods. Not a string of hair was on the blade, only a bunch of cream.

"Ouch," I shouted. "You cut me."

I knew what that meant, and Steven tossed the razor behind him. He squirted more cream in his mouth, and dove in to clean up his mess. He did get around to shaving me, and he stood behind me as we looked in the mirror to comment on my new look.

"I don't like it." I pouted. "It's too bald."

"Oh, I love it. It looks sexier, and now I can really see how fat and juicy it is."

I still disagreed, and after we took a quick shower, we got in bed to watch a movie. As soon as the movie started, the instant message sound on his laptop went off, letting him know that a message was waiting. He turned down the volume on the TV, and when he opened his laptop, he connected with Liz through the video Web camera.

"Hi," I could hear her saying.

"Hello," he said into the microphone. "I take it

you've been in meetings all day, since you're just now calling me?"

"I called earlier, but you didn't answer the phone. I left you a message. You didn't get it?"

"I haven't checked the messages yet."

"Well, I am so out of here tomorrow. I have been in meetings, but have made little progress. I can't wait to tell you about Mr. Aimes, and, baby, I am really considering quitting my job. If I do, will you support me on my decision? I'm getting so tired of the disorganization with this company, and it's starting to stress me."

"Of course I'll support you. You know we'll be okay financially, and if you need to take some time off work, do it."

"I knew you'd say that. It means a lot to me, and I can't wait to get out of here tomorrow. My plane leaves at 5:00 P.M., and I should be in St. Louis by eight. Can you pick me up at the airport?"

"No problem. Get some rest, baby, and I'll see you tomorrow."

"You get some rest too. Love you."

"Ditto."

Steven put the laptop on his nightstand, and if I didn't know any better, I would have thought that they had the perfect marriage. They were so cordial to each other, and there was no doubt in my mind that the love was definitely there. Basically, Steven had it made, but all of the love that he seemed to have from Liz, I guess for him, wasn't enough. Greed was something else, and he had the best of any and everything he wanted. A lot of men did, and nothing personal, but I just wanted to make sure I had the best of everything too.

Since Liz was due back tomorrow, she cut my time with Steven by one full day. I had to make the best of it, and after the movie went off, we took a nap. The nap extended into the wee hours of the morning, and I was awakened from my sleep by Steven's roaming hands.

"Wake up," he whispered in my ear. We both lay sideways, but he was behind me. He lifted my leg over his, entering me from behind. We went at it for hours, until the sun had come up on us. By then, we were too tired to get out of bed, and had fallen back asleep in each other's arms.

I was knocked out, lying between Steven's legs. I heard him mumble something, but couldn't make out what he'd said.

"What did you say?" I asked in a groggy tone.

He yawned. "I . . . I said what's that smell."

"What smell?" I inhaled, but really couldn't smell anything. "I don't smell anything."

We lay silent for a minute, and then the smoke detectors in the house started going off.

My head jerked up from Steven's chest and he damn near threw me off of him. "That smell," he said. "The smell of smoke."

I was starting to smell it, and as I hurried out of the room after Steven, we could see the flames blazing in portions of the lower level.

"Oh my God," I yelled, covering my mouth. Steven quickly dialed 911, starting to panic.

"My house is on fire!" He said, breathing heavily. "Please send the fire department right away!"

He quickly hung up and pointed to my purse on the

dresser. "Get your purse. Don't know if you have time to put on any clothes, but let's get the hell out of here!"

We scurried around the room, and, unable to find my clothes, I opted for Steven's robe. I grabbed my purse, and when he opened a window, I cocked my head back.

"No way," I said, as I wasn't up to jumping out of a two-story window.

He took my hand. "We may not have a choice."

As we hurried out of the bedroom, we saw that the front entrance was covered with smoke and fire. Luckily for us, there was another set of stairs that led to the kitchen. That stairway was smoky, but we didn't see any flames. Steven continued to hold my hand as we ran through the kitchen and exited through the back door. We were coughing like crazy and my eyes were slightly burning. When we got outside, we stepped as far away from the house as we could, watching the fire as it was quickly increasing.

"Are you okay?" Steven asked while looking at me, and at his burning house. We could hear the fire trucks coming. A part of him was still in a panicked state, yet he seemed calm.

"I . . . I think so."

"Go. Go get in your car and leave. I don't know what the hell happened, but I know my neighbors are going to be coming outside to see what's up."

I nodded and hurried down the street to get in my car. I could barely catch my breath. This was definitely a déjà vu moment for me. Who in the hell could have done this? I just knew that Drake was going to jump up out of nowhere to do something to me, but even so, when someone pulled the back of my ponytail and held my head steady, I was caught off guard. I couldn't even see who it was in my rearview mirror, because the person in the back seat had turned the mirror in another direction. The grip on my hair was so tight that I couldn't move my head if I tried. I felt the sharp blade touching my neck and I squeezed my eyes together. My stomach was tied in knots, and my chest was heaving up and down. I didn't know if it was time for me to see the white light.

"If you move or say anything, I will cut your fucking throat," she said. I recognized her voice, and, yes, it was Liz. "I've known about your trifling tail for months, Chase, and when you stated that no man was off limits, I started to watch you. You were so right about my husband, and even though I accepted the fact that he was a whore, I could in no way put up with him allowing you to come into my home and fuck him in my bed.

"Just who in the hell do you think you are, bitch! Was the dick that damn good where you had to run up into my house when I wasn't at home to get it?"

Liz pushed my head forward, then snapped it back. I didn't know if she was trying to break my neck, but it sure as hell felt like it. She pressed the blade into my neck even harder. "I bet you didn't think I would go this far, did you? And in case you didn't, let me tell you something. My husband's dick belongs to me, not you. So you rented it out for a while, and now, your lease is up. Your time will not be extended, and if you ever pursue Steven again, I will kill you, and dump your useless body in the trash where it belongs. I intend to watch Steven's every move, and if he goes anywhere near you, I will slice his dick off and send it to you by mail. Only because I don't play crazy, Chase, I am. Consider yourself warned, and from this day forward, my goddamn husband is off limits!"

Liz's cell phone rang, and she let go of my hair. She kept the blade next to my throat, daring me to move. Now, I was no fool. I had been to her level before, and Plan B was telling me to keep my butt still.

Her voice calmed and Liz was polite as ever.

"Hello," she said, pausing for a long time. "Oh, honey, no. Please don't tell me that." She paused again. "How bad is it and are you okay?" I could hear Steven saying something, but Liz cut him off. "I'm leaving right now. Stay at the house and I will take a taxi from the airport. I love you and I am so glad that you're okay." She paused. "Okay, bye."

She removed the blade from my neck, but I jumped, not knowing if she intended to jab me with it. "I mean what I said, Chase. To think, a few days ago, I was going to let you keep Steven. I changed my mind, because I need to make sure there are more consequences for his actions. You don't need to worry yourself about him, okay? A man who cheats will always pay the price, and he will have to put out thousands of dollars for repairing our lovely home. I'm taking some time off work, and it's going to be fun to watch him repair all of the damage he's done. I doubt that he'll have time to entertain you, but trust me, you do not want to see me under these circumstances again. Have a nice life, and just make sure that it never again interferes with mine."

Liz opened the back door and got out. I started the car and slowly drove off. I straightened the rearview mirror and, as I looked at her in it, I couldn't help but take a deep breath and smile. First, because I was still alive. Second, because I had finally come face-to-face with a woman as bold as me. I definitely liked her style, and sooner or later, Steven was going to have to pay up. As much as I was going to miss him, it was time to kiss that dick good-bye. In no way was I up to battling with a woman who was capable of burning down her own house, and Liz was definitely one bad bitch. Besides, maybe this was a sign for me to think about redeeming myself. As I looked back at all I'd done, I could have made better choices that would have never led me to this point. Lance was a decent person to talk to, and seeing him on a professional level may be a good idea to get me on the right track. It would be awhile before I could come up with a Plan B to replace Steven, but knowing me, I'd come up with something.

I quickly made my way out of their subdivision, trying to avoid the police who had blocked a nearby intersection. My car was almost on empty, so I pulled over to the nearest gas station to fill my tank. I still had on nothing but Steven's robe, and hesitated to get out and pump the gas dressed as I was. When I spotted Korey's car parked by a nearby pay phone, I knew his timing couldn't be more right. I pulled my car next to his, but he wasn't inside. I figured he was inside of the gas station getting something, so I waited inside of my car until he came out. My eyes searched his car, and when I noticed what looked to be gasoline containers on the back seat, I exited my car to get a closer look. I started to put two and two together, and just my luck, his cell phone was vibrating on the front seat. I opened his car door, and I looked to see who the caller was; it was Liz. She had sent him a text and it read:

TNKS 4 UR HLP, BOO. I OWE U, & I WILL PAY MY SEX DEBT TO U 2MORRO NIGHT. I HAVE SOOO N-JOYED THESE LAST MONTHS 2GETHER AND I KNEW IT WOULD BE WORTH IT! HA! THEY DN'T HAV A CLUE!

I dropped the phone on the ground, puzzled by what I suspected. Liz and Korey had hooked up too! No wonder she was so upset with me that day in her office. It explained Korey's ability to move on so quickly. I couldn't believe his ass was willing to set me on fire. After all the good sex I had given him, how in the hell could he? He was messing with the wrong woman, and Liz had definitely met her match.

Korey was still inside, and as mad as I was, I wasn't worried about the cameras seeing me. If I had to, this was one time I'd go to court and defend myself for my actions. He attempted to burn me first, and I was defending myself from a man who was stalking me. Yeah, that sounded about right, and to hell with redemption right now. I shook the gasoline cans on his back seat to see if any octane remained inside. There was enough to do what I had to do, and after I poured the gas on his seats, I removed the matches from my purse. I knew the flames would quickly ignite, so I hurried to toss several lit matches inside of his car. I tightened Steven's robe, and dressed as I was, I made my way inside of the gas station. Korey was sitting on a stool, talking to a lady who was making a shake and burger behind the counter.

I stepped up to him, and when he turned his head and saw me, he looked as if he'd seen a ghost. I took a seat on the stool next to him.

"Can I get a burger with extra cheese and mayo?" I said to the lady behind the counter. She looked at what I had on, and then glanced at Korey. Before she or he could say anything, a woman came inside, yelling at the top of her lungs.

"Oh, my God! Someone's car is on fire! It's starting to spread all over!"

I smirked, while looking into Korey's eyes. He quickly wised up, but before he could get out of his seat, I grabbed his sack, gripping it as tightly as I could.

"You lousy bastard," I said, tightening my grip on his balls. "When you talk to your bitch again, make sure you tell her it's on. As far as I'm concerned, her marriage to Steven is over, thanks to this little game the two of you played. He's going to love to hear about this, and I just may have my screwing buddy back after all. Meanwhile, if you ever come near me again, the only dick that will be cut off and mailed to her is yours!"

I let go of Korey's package, and his voice screeched, but he was in so much pain, nothing came out. He staggered away from the counter before dropping to his knees. Before the police and fire department came, I got the hell out of there. I wasn't sure if my photo from the cameras would make the news or not, and if I had some explaining to do, so be it. As a matter of fact, I figured it would be in my best interest to call my cousin, who was an attorney, just in case.

I drove off the parking lot, but turned to look at

Korey as he observed the hot flames blazing from his car. He slammed his hat on the ground, shaking his head in disbelief. I smiled, having no regrets about Steven, Korey, or Drake. I learned that in my case, I had to do what was necessary and doable for me. I thought hard about Liz, and pertaining to her, I'd have to come up with a more vicious and masterfully put-together Plan B.